HARD RIDE

LESSONS IN DOMINANCE

JACKIE ASHENDEN

I came looking for closure. He offered me one night.

And he brought backup.

Katherine

I didn't expect to see my ex-husband on The Club App —bearded, commanding, and very much a Dom. Curiosity got the best of me, and now I'm standing inside his private club...with no idea what I'm about to say yes to. Tate has always known how to push my buttons—but when his best friend Lucas joins in? Let's just say one night won't be nearly enough.

Tate

I let her go once. I won't do it again. Now she's here, in my world, asking for a taste. So I'm going to give her everything she ran from—and more. And if that means sharing her with my best friend for one unforgettable night? She won't walk out of here the same.

Lucas

I've wanted her for years. I just never crossed the line— because she was Tate's. But now she's ours. And I'll do everything I can to make sure one night turns into forever.

1

Katherine

I'm at the bar having a drink with Laurel, one of my co-workers, when I see it. She's turning to answer a question from the guy sitting on the other side of her, and her phone is on the bar top. It's unlocked since she was typing something in it, and I just happened to glance over at the screen.

Whatever app she's looking at is still open, and right there, staring back at me, is my ex-husband's face.

For a second, all I feel is shock. Then I think that maybe I made a mistake. But fuck, there's no mistaking him.

It's Tate. Tate O'Rourke.

My breath catches. Nothing like an unexpected glimpse of your ex ten years after you left him to really make a girl feel alive. I glance away, conscious that my heart is racing, which it shouldn't. I left him a long time ago, never intending to see him again, not after the way we left things, so I have no idea why my attention keeps getting dragged back to the picture on Laurel's phone.

Tate's looking away from the camera, but you can see his features. They're harder than I remember, grimmer, too. He's got a neatly trimmed black beard — which he never had when we were married — but the straight, black brows and short black hair are the same. His green eyes are looking elsewhere, as if someone is talking to him out of shot, but I remember those green eyes, too. Always so intense, burning with a fury that I guess he was entitled to considering his shitty upbringing, but there was also a demand there as well, that I didn't understand. He always wanted more than I could give.

There *is* something different about him in this photo, something indefinable. A presence he didn't have when we were married, and even in the picture, I can sense it. It's something authoritative, something charismatic, something...

Shit, I really should stop staring at him.

"So you see it too, right?"

I blink, then try to pretend that I haven't been looking at her phone, because that damn man doesn't affect me, not anymore. "Oh? What?"

Laurel, naturally, sees right through me and grins. "Come on, I know you were staring." She picks up her phone and holds it out to me, Tate's face staring from the screen. "Because I don't blame you. That guy is fire."

Laurel doesn't know about my ill-fated one-year marriage back when I was nineteen. I don't tell anyone about it, because why? It was years ago, and I've moved on.

I very determinedly do not look at Tate's face again. "Yes," I say. "He really is. So what is this?" I gesture at the screen. "A new dating app?"

Laurel gives me the world's most secretive smile. "Kind of. It's called The Club." She leans in, whispering. "It matches up kinky people."

Ugh. I'd never shame anyone for their sexy choices, but kink is very definitely not for me. I'm totally vanilla and I prefer it that way.

"Right," I say. "Good for them."

"It's BDSM mainly," Laurel clarifies, even though I don't need her to clarify. "But there are other kinds of kink on the app."

"Is that what you're into?" I raise a brow. "You kept that quiet."

She laughs. "I'm not sure if that's something I want to explore yet, but I heard about the app from someone at work and was kind of intrigued. Apparently, it's very safe. There's lots of vetting done on everyone who wants to sign up, you know, regular STD tests etcetera, etcetera."

"How romantic," I mutter. I'm not actually judging. I mean, if you're into all that stuff, then you'd want to be physically safe, but for me, it's all way too clinical.

Laurel ignores me in favor of waving her phone in my face. "Come on, look at this man. Is he, or is he not, hot AF?"

Since she's leaving me with no choice, I peer reluctantly

at the screen. Yep, there's Tate, and below his photo is a very simple bio. It lists only his BDSM experience and a list of all the things he's into sexually.

He's a Dom. What a surprise. Not.

Even ten years ago he was a bossy asshole in bed, and I didn't like it. He scared me with the way he took charge, and not that I was scared for my safety or anything — Tate was never a man who would hurt a woman — it was more that I found it...deeply uncomfortable. Mainly for reasons I never told anyone about because I was too young. Suffice to say, they involved one of my mother's hook-ups and my mother calling me a filthy little slut.

Laurel regards me from her barstool. "You're interested," she says. "I can tell."

I am not interested. In fact, the depths to which I'm not interested cannot be measured, and I want to tell her that. Except I can feel my face heating like a teenage girl's and it's very irritating — one of the 'perks' of being a pale-skinned redhead — especially when there's no reason for it.

"I'm not." I try to sound *extremely* casual.

"Liar. You liked that guy's picture a lot."

I've known Laurel since law school. She's with a corporate law firm in Midtown, while I'm with Harlow and Nelson, divorce lawyers to New York's rich and famous. She thinks I need to get out and meet someone, because she's worried about my current sex drought. I, on the other hand, am not worried about it. I can take or leave sex, to be honest, and anyway, work takes up most of my time. I don't need Laurel hooking me up with anyone on some stupid kink app.

Come on, it's Tate. Tate O'Rourke.

So what? I'm over him and over all the horrible,

confusing feelings that consumed me back then. I've got no desire to revisit them.

If Tate's on that app, Lucas is probably on it too.

Oh shit, that's true. Lucas Thorne, Tate's best friend and mine.

"Yeah, he's okay," I say noncommittally.

Laurel frowns at me, then looks down at her phone. "Your gauge is busted. He certainly makes me want to sign up in a heartbeat."

I should tell her not to get anywhere near him, because he was a whole thing ten years ago, and I'm sure he still is. I mean, I had to leave without telling him, because I didn't want him to follow me. And he would have. Both of them would have.

Every so often, I'll look him up on the internet, mainly for nosiness reasons, and every time I do, he seems to have gone from strength to strength.

He was into engineering back when I knew him, always tinkering around with cars and other machines. Now, he and Lucas own an airplane company that builds fantastically engineered and expensive private planes for rich people. O'Rourke and Thorne Aeronautics.

Laurel gives me a speculative look as she glances back up from the phone again. "I've got an idea."

Oh, God, no. It's never a good thing when Laurel has an 'idea'.

"Perhaps we can talk about that—" I begin.

"The Club actually has a venue in Manhattan," she interrupts. "It opened last week and they have a night for people new to the scene."

I tense, because I know what she's going to say. She's going to say 'let's go down and check it out' and I'll have to refuse, because there's no way I'm going to a sex club.

"I'm not sure I'd be into it," I say. "I don't want to be bossed around by some asshole."

"You don't have to be if that's not what you want." Laurel has that gleam in her eye, the one she gets when she's taken an idea and is running the fuck away with it. "I bet there's all kinds of other things there you might be into."

"Lor—"

"*He* might be there." Laurel gives me a meaningful look.

I blink. Tate? Here in New York? His company is based in California, I'm sure of it.

"Uh, why?" I ask stupidly.

"Because he's based in New York, according to the app. And if he's on The Club app, I bet he'll be at The Club itself."

I want to tell her that's an excellent reason *not* to go anywhere near The Club itself, yet five minutes later, we're both sitting in an Uber as it makes its way Downtown.

I can't quite believe I'm coming with her, but sometimes Laurel is impossible to resist. She told me that even if I wasn't interested in anything at The Club, she was, and that she needed me to be her emotional support vanilla.

It's definitely not because I want to see Tate again. I absolutely do *not* want to see Tate again. I never ever think of him, even, so it's not as if I'm still love with him. Or with Lucas.

Besides, even if by some evil miracle they're there, I'll just leave before they can spot me. They'll probably have forgotten me anyway. It was a long time ago, and they're rich as hell, not to mention extremely hot. They'll have models and movie stars hanging off their arms and won't be at all interested in some freckled redhead they once knew ten years ago.

The Club is nothing like the sex club I was expecting as

we pull up outside. In fact, it doesn't look like a club at all. It's a historic mansion, with old gas lamps on the facade, stone columns, and wrought iron balustrades. There's no sign anywhere, just a gold plaque on the wall beside the big double doors.

A couple of normal-looking people dressed in normal clothes approach, then disappear inside. They don't look super kinky, so maybe it won't be wall-to-wall vinyl corsets and gimp suits inside.

"Wow," Laurel mutters as we get out of the Uber. "This is *not* what I expected."

"No," I say, still half thinking through some excuses to go home.

The door is standing open, though, and when we step inside, it's into a wide, ornate hallway. It could be the old hallway of years gone by, with thick carpet, chandeliers, and high ceilings with ornate cornices. A pair of red velvet curtains are drawn at one end of it.

A beautiful woman with black hair, wearing a tight, red silk gown, is standing behind an antique desk. She smiles at Laurel and me as we enter. "Welcome to The Club," she says. "I'm Claire. Are you members?"

"No," Laurel says. "But I have the app. It's newbie night, right?"

"It is, and also, ladies are free of charge."

I can hear music coming from behind those curtains, nothing too loud or brash, just something with a pulsing, driving beat. Nerves are starting to collect in my gut, and I'm beginning to regret coming here. I'm not super sexual or anything, plus I don't know anything about sex clubs, so I'm hoping it's not going to be sex shows and whipping. I really don't want to watch that kind of thing.

Claire gives us a rundown on The Club and what's not

allowed inside, which includes our phones. We're also given white rubber bracelets that Claire tells us to wear at all times. They denote our newbie status and mean no one will approach us. We can explore safely without being bothered.

Not being bothered sounds ideal, but I've already decided I'm not going to explore anything at all. I'm going to hang near the entrance so I can escape if I need to.

Nothing at all to do with Tate or Lucas. Nothing.

Once Clair has finished her spiel, she leads us down the hallway and pulls back one of the curtains. "Enjoy, ladies," she says.

And we step inside The Club.

2

Tate

There's nothing like fucking in front of an audience. It's a high I particularly enjoy, especially with a vocal sub letting you know how much she's enjoying the fucking. Everyone watching wants to be her, everyone wants my cock, and they all want to be in my power, whether they know it or not.

It's why they can't look away.

The sub I'm fucking tonight is experienced, and I've

played with her before. We're giving a graphic demonstration for people who are new to the scene and want to explore what The Club Manhattan has to offer in a safe way.

We pride ourselves on safety at The Club.

I visited the original Club out in Oakland a couple of years ago, and I enjoyed it so much that I offered to start one here in Manhattan. The Club's managers were all in, especially given the level of funds I have at my disposal.

We opened last week, and sign-ups to the app have been brisk, while The Club itself is full most nights. We cater to everyone's legal sexual tastes, with an emphasis on BDSM, and we also have an excellent bar. It's elite, this place. More like a wine bar with sex than vinyl and plastic with a stripper pole (though we have one of those too).

Right now, I'm on the stage with the sub bent over a bench. She's naked, her hands cuffed at the small of her back. I've got a good grip on her cuffs, holding on as I fuck her with the kind of care and precision that I like to bring to every scene.

Tonight, I've kept the equipment to a minimum, concentrating more on the psychological aspects of BDSM and the power exchange, since that's really what newbies need to know before they start playing around with a pair of handcuffs. Also, new Doms need a good example to follow, and I like to take an instructional role.

Lucas, my best friend and business partner, is standing to the side of the stage, keeping an eye on the crowd. He's the monitor for our first newbies night, since he's also invested in The Club, and he likes rules. He doesn't look like rules are his thing, but they are, and most especially the safety of everyone in the club. We have other monitors keeping an eye out, but everyone knows Lucas is in charge tonight.

The sub is wailing — Cherry's in fine form — and she's nice and tight around my cock. But the only one getting off will be her. If you want me to come, you have to earn it, and Cherry's been a touch too bratty tonight. She won't be complaining, though. She's had two orgasms already, and she's looking down the barrel of a third, so she'll be well satisfied. I'm not the only one who likes an audience.

I grip her cuffs tighter, using them as leverage to work deeper, hitting that spot inside her that I know makes her scream even louder, and she does. She's like a fucking air raid siren, and it's music to my ears. I take one hand away from the cuffs, reaching around to give her clit a pinch, thrusting hard as I do, and she screams the house down, the pulse of her pussy around my cock signaling she's done.

I give her a few moments to catch her breath, then I pull out, disposing of the condom in the bin provided. Condoms aren't needed with Cherry and me — we're both fully up to date with clinic visits and birth control — but I like to provide an example of safe sex for the new crowd.

I tuck my cock away, ignoring the fact that it's still hard, zip myself up, then I see to the sub's restraints. I take my time examining her to make sure she's okay and not harmed, as any self-respecting Dom will do, telling the crowd that's what I'm doing as I do it.

Master Killian comes up on stage to grab Cherry and take her somewhere quiet for some aftercare, since I've got some other things to do. She prefers Killian to do it. He's gentler than I am.

The newbies are wide-eyed as I step down from the stage, some of them backing away slightly, reacting unconsciously to my authority. I always like that, the deference. I don't expect it in real life, though once you have enough money and power, you get it anyway, but in The Club, it's a kick, and I require it.

Many of the crowd are eyeing me with undisguised interest, but I'm not initiating some untried newbie into the scene tonight. I'm in demonstration mode, so if anyone's getting fucked, it's only the experienced subs who signed up to do demos, not anyone else.

Lucas comes up beside me, making sure the crowd keeps their distance. Then, he gives his little lecture on Club rules, especially the "no touching unless permission is given" rule. Some people need plenty of reminders.

I make my way to the large alcove down the back of the club, where the Dominants tend to gather. A huge, black leather sectional sofa lines the walls of the space, with a couple of low coffee tables in the center. Mistress Nell is there, sipping a martini, looking fine in her tight leather corset dress and six-inch red stilettos. She's going to be providing a Domme demonstration, and she's on stage next.

"Looking good, Tate," she purrs as I sit down. Scott, one of her subs, is behind the bar, and he'll no doubt be getting me the vodka neat that I like after a scene. "If you're not careful, someone might want to introduce you to the joys of being a switch."

Relaxing back against the couch, I smile at her. This is an old game we play, and we both enjoy it since neither of us has a submissive bone in our bodies. "Sure," I say. "Ladies first."

She gives a delightfully dirty laugh. "You're such a tease. Looks like a good crowd tonight, though."

I glance over at the stage and the newbies surrounding Lucas, listening intently as he explains the club rules. It's a sea of white bracelets, naturally.

"Yeah, not bad for the first night," I say, smiling at Scott as he approaches with my drink. He smiles back but lowers his eyes in deference as he places it on the table in front of me. "Thanks," I say, and then, to reward him, I add, "Your sub has very pretty manners, Mistress Nell."

Nell is clearly pleased, and so is Scott by the looks of his grin as he turns away. "And a very pretty cock too," she says, watching admiringly as he leaves.

Only the performers giving the demonstrations are in their fetish gear tonight. When he's behind the bar, Scott normally wears a pair of tight leather trousers and nothing else, and when he's not behind the bar, it's a leash and a cock ring. Now, though, he's in formal black slacks and a black T-shirt.

Nell takes another sip of her drink, eyeing the crowd. It's newbies only, so most of the regulars aren't here, which is fine. But for the kinky among us, everyone's very conscious of themselves and their roles, so the atmosphere is different. It's more constrained. No one wants to scare the horses, so to speak.

Nell and I talk shop for a few minutes, then she puts down her drink. "Show time," she says and rises gracefully to her feet. She's small, but her authority packs a punch, and it's on full display as she stalks towards the stage. Her other sub, Amy, is already kneeling there, waiting.

At the end of the night, Lucas and I will meet with the others on the team to talk about how the night went, and I'll get some numbers. I'd like this to be a regular event so there's a safe space for people new to the scene. Nothing like exposure to be good for a business, after all.

I'm still sipping meditatively at my vodka, watching Nell do her thing and the crowd's reactions, when my attention strays to the bar area, a flash of red catching my eye.

I don't have a type, per se, but I do have a certain...weakness for redheads. And that is indeed a redhead sitting at my bar. She's small and neat in her corporate suit of dark gray, her hair in a tight bun on the back of her head. She's sitting with another woman, her head turned away so I can't see her face. The other woman, a blonde, is also wearing a suit, so they must have just come from work, or maybe after-work drinks. A spur of the moment visit, likely enough. But the redhead is...familiar.

I narrow my gaze, studying her, and then it hits me, the impact like a fucking crossbow bolt to my chest.

It's Katherine. *My* Katherine. After so many fucking years, here she is. At my fucking bar. In my fucking club. What the hell is she doing here? Did she see me just now on the stage? Does she know that I'm here at all? Is that *why* she's here?

But no, she can't have seen me, of course not. She wouldn't be sitting on that goddamn barstool so comfortably if she had.

I've never forgotten how she walked out on me ten years ago, and without so much as a damn word. I was too demanding, too intense, and too young back then to know how to deal with either myself or her, so I had to let her go.

But after ten years and a fuck ton of growing, both mentally and emotionally, I know myself better now. I channel my demands and my intensity into the boardroom and into the dungeon, where they're valued and needed, where people want them, where they get off on them, and where I can indulge myself in a safe way that won't hurt anyone.

No, I've never forgotten how she walked out.

I've never forgotten her.

After she left, I swore to myself that when I was ready, I would find her. I would convince her that I was different, that I'd changed, and I still wanted to be with her. And I am different in a way. But my essential nature is still the same: I'm Dominant. Possessive. Controlling. And in the dungeon, I can be who I am, with people who are the right kind of afraid, and I won't ever conform myself for another person's comfort again.

Which means I should stay where I am on the couch. I should definitely not approach her in any way, because if she couldn't handle me ten years ago, she definitely couldn't handle me now.

But then I see her freeze on her barstool, every muscle of her tight, and her friend has noticed and is putting a concerned hand on her shoulder. Yet Katherine shakes her friend's hand off, and slides from her seat as if looking for escape, and I know all at once why she wants to escape.

She's seen Lucas.

Except he's standing in the crowd, blocking the exit, and if she wants to leave, she'll draw attention, so she goes in the opposite direction.

Towards me.

3

Katherine

Holy fucking shit. My heart is racing, fight or flight kicking in. I didn't think when I slipped off the barstool; all I wanted was to escape. Because Lucas Thorne *is* here, of course, he fucking is, and it's just my luck that he saw me.

We must have come in just after something had happened on the stage, because there were plenty of people milling about in front of it, and a couple of guys dressed in black moving strange looking furniture around on it.

Inside the club, it's less mansion and more Moulin Rouge, with low lighting, red velvet couches, a long wooden bar, and lots of alcoves with red velvet curtains.

It's luxurious, giving off decadent vibes, and again, not what I expected a sex club to be like. Especially with all the apparently normal people standing around, all in business casual, midriff tops, and cocktail dresses.

I could have been in any high-priced Manhattan bar.

I mean, that was until a small woman in a corset dress and sky-high stilettos, her black hair in ponytail on the top of her head, started strutting over to the stage, and I noticed the naked woman in handcuffs kneeling on it waiting for her.

I'd been studiously *not* looking at the stage before that — Laurel had been too busy downloading her excitement to me anyway — and so it was only when the crowd started pushing towards it that I'd taken a sneaky glimpse and noticed the man standing in the middle of the crowd of people wearing white bracelets.

Tall, over six two. Wearing dark blue pants with a white business shirt, the top few buttons undone. His hair under the lights was a dark tawny, streaks of gold and toffee threaded through it, and he was to-die-for-beautiful. A fallen angel's face.

I remembered that face. Impossible to forget. The light to Tate's dark, his best friend and mine, and the huge complication in our marriage.

Lucas.

I'd frozen on my barstool, absolutely in shock, barely processing his presence, and he must have sensed me looking, because abruptly, he glanced in my direction.

And I'd felt the impact of his stare like a blow, the same kind of impact I'd experienced back in the bar, when I'd seen Tate's picture. His eyes had widened with shock, flaring brilliant gold, and then just as quickly, they'd narrowed.

I panicked, not going to lie, and I'm still panicking as I head away from the stage, into a dimmer, darker area of the club. Laurel is calling my name, but I don't turn. I just want to get away.

It's a dumb move because the exit is now behind me, and I should have run in that direction, because surely Lucas wouldn't have chased me out onto the street. We only shared a fleeting glimpse of each other, and that might not have been recognition on his face at all. Maybe he was just shocked to see someone so determinedly vanilla in the club or something?

Then again, who knows? One thing's for sure. If he's here, then Tate must be here too.

I'm hoping there's a door down this way, to the bathrooms or offices or something that I could slip through, but there doesn't seem to be any exits, fuck it. There's a dark alcove, though, so maybe I could hide myself in a corner of it.

Except now I'm getting closer, I see a man sitting there, and he's rising slowly to his feet, and he's so tall, so fucking tall. He's wearing an immaculate three-piece suit in a dark gray, with a white shirt and a blue silk tie, and he stands there almost as if he's waiting for me, immovable as a mountain.

And my body knows exactly who this is, even as it takes a couple of seconds for my brain to catch up, because I feel an intense rush of fear, desire, anger, and happiness all rolled into one.

It's Tate, and my feet are still moving, and I can't seem to stop them until I'm right at the alcove, and he's in front of me. That face I saw a mere couple of hours ago on Laurel's screen is right *there*. Roughly handsome, with a hard, gritty edge. A mouth that feels softer than it looks. Black hair and beard. And forbidding, my God, *so* forbidding.

He looks like a dark god crafted by an ancient civilization.

An avenging god.

I'm so fucked.

He says nothing, simply gazes at me, and I realize then that the picture on the app hasn't done him justice. It captured only a fraction of his...presence. His charisma. The intense force of what I can only assume is his authority.

It hits me like a wave, and my instinctive response is to turn around and run like hell back the way I came. Except when I turn, I discover that following right behind me is Lucas, amber eyes blazing, broad shoulders completely blocking my view of the exit. He stops and folds his muscular arms, standing there like a beautiful golden wall.

"Katherine," Tate says from behind me, his familiar voice somehow darker, more gravelly, and much more certain than I remember. "Please, sit down."

I feel cornered, hunted. I'm trapped like prey between two lions, both of whom could tear me apart so easily. Who *did* tear me apart years ago, and it took me a good couple of years to get over them. But I *am* over them, and even though it's too late to pretend they haven't seen me or apparently forgotten me, I'm not going to run like a coward. I couldn't handle either of them back when I was younger, but I'm not the same woman I was back then. I'm stronger, more sure of myself, and I'm not confused about my feelings, not anymore. Also, if either of them tries any of that Dom shit on me, I'll kick them in the nuts.

I take a moment to push the panic away and collect myself, then I smirk at Lucas before turning around to face my ex-husband.

"Tate," I say dryly. "Fancy meeting you here."

He doesn't smile. The light is so dim that the green of his eyes is lost, but I see them glitter. "Yes," he says. "Likewise. Like I said, please, sit."

"No, thank you." I'm glad at how steady my voice is. "I'm only here with my friend. We're going in a minute."

Tate looks past me, towards the bar area, then his gaze comes back to mine again. "Your friend is watching Mistress Nell on the stage. She's more than happy."

I turn around again, trying to spot Laurel, but Lucas prowls closer, and I can't see past him. Strangely, my heart is still racing, and my entire body feels suddenly alive and alert. It's as if it knows I'm in danger, yet I'm not afraid. There's a kind of breathless anticipation rushing through me instead, and I have no idea why.

I decide to ignore both it and Lucas as I turn back to Tate. "Again," I say, attempting the same dry tone. "While I'd love to go over old times and reminisce, that's a no, thank you."

Tate's smile flashes, white in the darkness of his beard, but it's not a pleasant smile. "I wasn't asking."

My body shivers at the flat note in his voice. It's a familiar feeling. I used to feel it back when we were together when he'd ask me to get him something or do something in a certain tone. I used to react badly to those orders— and they *were* orders — because I hated that shiver and how it seemed to reach something deep inside me. A part of me that liked it. But that part is gone now, so there's no reason for me to be shivering like a wet dog simply because he said something.

"Too fucking bad," I say, not caring how rude I sound.

Tate doesn't react, only glancing over my shoulder at his friend standing behind me. "Give us a moment, Luc."

Immediately, the feeling of pressure at my back disappears.

"Katherine," Tate says in the same authoritative tone. "Sit."

I'm fully intending to tell him to fuck off, so I'm barely aware that I'm doing exactly what he says until I find myself sitting on the black leather sectional that lines the alcove. Shit. How did that happen?

Tate sits opposite me, a tumbler on the coffee table in front of him. It's half full of a clear liquid. Seems he still likes vodka, though I bet it's a more expensive brand these days.

His eyes gleam, but he says nothing immediately, which is infuriating.

"All right," I say, crossing one leg over the other, trying to act as if I sat down of my own accord and not in response to him. "So, you want to talk."

"And you want to obey." He says it conversationally, without any emphasis at all, yet I feel each word echo inside of me like the tolling of a bell, which is actually insane.

My cheeks heat, and it's pretty fucking annoying, because of course, he'll be able to see even in the dim lighting in the alcove. "Jesus, Tate," I say. "That's quite the conversation opener after ten years."

"But that's why you're here, isn't it?" He regards me, eyes glittering. "In this club. On newbie night."

Seriously? He's leading with this? No 'hi, how are you' or 'what have you been doing in the decade since we last met' or even 'God, what are *you* doing here?' No, it's straight into what presumably is Dom bullshit.

And you obeyed without even thinking about it.

No, I didn't. I was going to sit down anyway. It's timing, that's all.

Anyway, it's unsurprising that he should be intense like this. He was back in high school when I first met him. I'd dropped my lunch tray in the school cafeteria, and he'd helped me clean it up, and the moment his eyes met mine, I was lost. Real lightning bolt, love at first sight stuff. Then, he'd directed that intensity at everyone and everything, his shitty home life giving him an angry edge.

Now, though, I can sense the change in him. I can see it. His intensity is still there, but it's been concentrated, controlled, directed. He's fully in charge of it now, and totally in command, and that angry edge has gone.

He's just as mesmerizing as he was back then, maybe even more so now, and my stupid heartbeat is working over-time with joy at seeing him. Traitor.

I'm not falling into that murky, confusing, awful place I got into with him again, though. I loved him, but I couldn't handle him. I couldn't handle his wild moods, his darkness, his anger, and neither could he. We were bad for each other, and that wasn't even counting my feelings for Lucas, too. So, I left. I had to. But leaving them both ripped my heart out, and I'm not going to put myself in that position again. I learn from my mistakes.

"Shouldn't we be having a civilized conversation first?" I ask, meeting his gaze head-on, letting him know he can't browbeat me. "I mean, we haven't seen each other for—"

"Ten years, I know." He tilts his head, studying me intently. "I always meant to find you again, Katherine."

My mouth dries. "What?"

"I've never forgotten you." His tone level, his voice deep and dark, and I know from the blaze in his eyes that he's telling me the truth. "I always knew you'd come back to me somehow, and here you are."

I feel like a tuning fork being struck; every part of me is vibrating. But with shock. I don't even know what to say.

Ten years and apparently, he hasn't forgotten me.

You haven't forgotten him, either.

I wish I could still lie to myself and say I had, yet sitting opposite him, his presence pulling at me like the moon pulls at the tides, it's too late for happy little lies.

Of course, I haven't forgotten him. How could I? He came into my life all those years ago, blazing like a comet, and I was dazzled. I was the good girl with the perfect grades, trying to be better than my alcoholic mother. Trying not to let her hold me back. I obeyed the rules. I was never out after curfew.

Then Tate appeared, the new guy at high school with the bad reputation. How his father was a meth head, beat him routinely, and how he stole cars, drank beer, smoked cigarettes, and vandalized property. The whole bad boy nine yards. He was a wild, thrilling presence, and all the girls used to follow him around like puppy dogs. But he only had eyes for me.

He's looking at me that way now, as if there's nothing more interesting in his world than me, only this time his gaze is even more intense than it used to be. Like a laser, boring into me.

"I...." My voice catches embarrassingly, and I have to clear my throat. "I'm not here for you, Tate," I manage firmly.

"Yes, you are." His mouth curves, intense gaze seeing right through me. "I'm exactly why you're here."

The part of me that I loathe trembles, but I shove that part back down into the box it came from. "Oh yeah," I say sarcastically. "You know me, can't get enough of sex clubs."

He ignores this. "Aren't you curious? Don't you want to know what it's all about?"

"Don't tell me. You're going to offer to show me the ropes, aren't you?"

Again, he flashes me that smile, white and predatory. "If you like ropes, sure. But I think you'd prefer handcuffs."

Oh, I love handcuffs. Not. I had a boyfriend bring round a pink fluffy pair once, but that was a firm no from me. I don't want to be tied up, thank you very much.

"So let me get this straight," I say, not doing a very good job of hiding my irritation. "We haven't seen each other for years, and the first thing you do is pressure me for sex."

"I'm not pressuring you for anything you don't want to give, Katherine," he says mildly.

"Hard disagree," I say. "Why do you even want this? Why can't we have a conversation first?"

"A conversation?" he echoes. "You didn't want one ten years ago, so why bother now?"

My cheeks burn. "There were good reasons I didn't talk to you." Firstly, Lucas reasons. And secondly.... other reasons.

"There always are with you." He keeps staring at me, and finally, I see it, the flicker of anger in his eyes. "But let's not go back over old ground. You're here in my club on newbie night, and things are still...unresolved between us. So why not have a chance to resolve them?"

My mouth is dry. I need a drink or *something* to take the edge off the sharp, bright panic inside me. I don't want to talk about those 'unresolved things'. I didn't back then, and I don't want to now.

Yet even so, the memories of our time together in bed

are still fresh. The times when he held my wrists down on the mattress on either side of my head as he fucked me. How I would come so fast and so hard, I swear I almost lost consciousness, and how afterwards I just felt...dirty.

When I was sixteen, I wandered into the kitchen at home one morning, and there was a strange guy there making himself breakfast. I hadn't been surprised, Mom's hookups often ended up being around in the morning. But then he started chatting to me and flirting with me. He was hot, and no one had ever paid me attention before, so I flirted back. Then, before I knew what was happening, he pushed me up against the wall and tried to put his hand up my nightie while kissing me.

Mom had walked in at that moment and saw us, and while he got nothing more than a finger wag, I got called a little slut and was grounded for a month. For 'leading him on' apparently.

It was sexual assault, and even at the time, I knew what he'd done was wrong, but the worst part of it was that...I'd liked it. I'd liked how he'd pushed me against the wall, holding my wrists above my head so I couldn't do anything to stop him, how I was completely at his mercy.

It was wrong to like it, though, and for years I tried to pretend it had never happened. Until Tate came into my life with his intense, sexual energy. His hands around my wrists, holding them down onto the mattress so I couldn't move, had been the single most erotic moment of my life, and yet it was the most deeply fucked up moment, too. Because I didn't want that experience in the kitchen with that guy to define my whole sexuality, yet with Tate, it kept being reinforced.

I should have said something to him at the time, but I was nineteen and didn't know how to have that conversation. I could barely articulate my own confused feelings about sex, even to myself, and then with Lucas and how he made me feel added to the mix, it only got even more complicated.

I swallow, painfully aware of Tate sitting opposite. He's lounging there, in his three-piece suit, and it must be hand-made because it fits his proportions exactly. He's broader than he used to be, his shoulders wide, and his blue tie gleaming against his white shirt. He takes up space not only with his hard, muscular body but also with his presence, a kind of fierce, sexual charisma that feels impossible to resist.

Fuck. I shouldn't still feel this way about him, this kind of helpless, breathless, out of control excitement that grips me and refuses to let go. I

hated it back then and I hate it now, because I *don't* get off on being a helpless victim, not anymore.

4

Tate

My Katherine is very determined not to let me see her fear, but I see it in her pretty blue eyes all the same. That's a change. She used to wear her heart on her sleeve, and I always loved that about her. Her openness and honesty were her greatest strengths.

But there was one thing she wasn't open or honest about and that was sex. She never told me why she got scared sometimes, especially when I held her down or restrained her in any way. It frustrated the shit out of me, because I didn't want to hurt her or scare her, and yet I fucking knew something was wrong. I tried to talk to her about it, but she'd clam up or change the subject, and then I'd get angry, which didn't help.

Things are different now, however. I know how to manage myself, and I know how I can make her open up to me the way she couldn't back then. It'll be challenging for her, but then she's never shied away from a challenge because the other thing she used to be was brave.

Anyway, it's clear that the moment she headed towards the alcove where I was sitting, blindly running from Lucas, I knew she was here for me. Oh, she tried to protest, tried to tell me that she was only here with her friend, but she was looking at me the way she used to all those years ago, and I knew that fate had brought her here.

Lucas was standing behind her, blocking her exit, the two of us working in sync, the way we always do when we're in the club. He was furious, of course, that she was here at all, still disturbing our peace in the same way she did a decade ago.

I was already friends with Lucas when I met her. He was a foster kid in a shitty foster situation, and I was an angry kid with a shitty parent, and naturally we bonded, especially being new kids at the same high school.

Then Katherine appeared. She dropped her tray in the school cafeteria, food spilling everywhere, and I helped her clean it all up. She smiled at me then, and said thank you, and it felt as if the sun had come inside and was shining on me. Her smile was bright, and her blue eyes, like a summer sky, were clear. I didn't see anything but her in that moment.

No one had ever thanked me for anything before, not

one fucking person, yet she had. And that smile... Christ, I would have done anything for that smile.

She was mine the moment I saw her.

Then I had to watch as she had the same effect on my best friend.

I know what he feels for her, what he's always felt for her, and while we've never talked about it, he's aware that I know his feelings, too. But I saw her first, so I have first claim, and that's just how it is. Lucas is not a man who takes another man's property, but he's not made of stone, either.

He was radiating anger when he stood behind her, so I told him to let Katherine and me have a few minutes so he could have some distance. I wanted to talk to her on my own anyway.

I'd really been going to open our conversation with something more standard, but when I told her to sit, and she sat like she was born to obey, I had to recalibrate. Refocus.

I RECOGNIZED THEN what I failed to see years ago, that she's likely to be a submissive and doesn't want to acknowledge it. She hasn't accepted her own responses the way I have, and even now, even after ten years, she's still afraid.

I can't have that. I can't have my bright, shining girl, who used to stand on the back of my motorcycle and pretend she was flying, be afraid.

"Tell me what scares you," I say, holding her gaze with mine. "And don't say you're not scared. I know you are."

She's sitting there primly, one leg over the other, neat as a new pin in her little suit and bun. I looked her up a few years ago and saw she'd gotten her law degree the way she always planned, and I was glad for her. She had a sharp intelligence and a way with words, and a determination to match, so it was no surprise. She looks like she's working in some firm somewhere, all buttoned up and prim, and I wonder if she enjoys it. I wonder if any other man has ever made her scream as loudly as I did.

Her hands are clasped in her lap, her full and pretty mouth tight as she rolls her eyes. "Seriously? You don't know me, Tate. I'm not the same person I was ten years ago."

"That's why I'm asking you now," I say. "If you were the same person, you wouldn't be anywhere near this club, let alone sitting on the couch opposite me." I lean forward and pick up my vodka, taking a leisurely sip. "Also, I'm not the same person, either."

Her gaze flickers under the pressure of mine, and she looks down at her hands. It's a submissive response, and it makes the Dom in me flex and stretch like a tiger waking from sleep. My cock is hardening again, and I'm conscious of the press of her breasts against her white shirt, and the neatness of her waist in her little suit skirt. She was the first pretty thing I ever had, the first pretty thing that was mine. Having her was like discovering a diamond in the waste-land, clear and glittering, untainted by all the shit that I had to deal with every day.

I wanted her to stay untainted and pure, to stay unafraid, and that's why I let her go. I didn't want to drag her down with me.

Except now, all I can think about is how pretty she'd look naked and in cuffs, kneeling at my feet.

"I don't know what you want me to say, Tate," she says impatiently. "I'm not afraid. I'm simply uninterested."

I almost laugh at that, because it's such a terrible lie. If she were uninterested, she wouldn't have obeyed my command and sat down. If she were uninterested, she wouldn't be checking me out the way she did just before, as if she can't drag her gaze away.

If she were uninterested, the pulse at the base of her throat wouldn't be racing, she wouldn't be flushed, and her pretty nipples wouldn't be hard.

"You don't have to be afraid of being submissive, Katherine," I say, deciding to ignore her lie. "We celebrate it here."

She scowls at me. "I'm not a submissive."

"Then why did you sit down when I told you to?"

"Because I was going to sit down anyway."

I just look at her, watching her blush deepen, her gaze flickering once again under the pressure of mine. "Now we both know you're lying," I murmur.

She rolls her eyes again. "Oh, for God's sake."

"There's nothing wrong with being submissive," I say, amused at how desperately she's denying the truth. "I can't be who I am without a submissive partner.

"Oh, right, you're a Dom. Of course you are."

I ignore her sarcasm. "You remember what I was like all those years ago. I was a scary motherfucker, and I don't blame you for leaving. The dungeon was a lifesaver for me. It taught me how to manage and control myself. How to have what I want, but in a safe way for me and my sexual partners."

She gazes at me warily, and I let her study me. I let her see my honesty. I'm not hiding anything or holding anything back. What I demand of my subs, I demand of myself, because after all, the only way any of this works is through total honesty.

"That doesn't mean I still want you," she says, throwing the words at me like a challenge, and it *is* a challenge. Because of course she still wants me.

"Oh, Katherine." I give her a wolfish smile. "Come on, now."

She flushes even deeper, and I remember that flush. She could never hide it, not with her pale skin. "You remember those times?" I go on, keeping my voice low, pushing her a little. "When I held your hands down beside your head and I fucked you like that? You came so fast and so hard, you left me behind."

Her red lashes come down, veiling her gaze. Her knuckles are white in her lap, and I know she remembers. She remembers every second.

"Have you ever come like that again?" I ask softly, pushing her further. "Have you ever screamed anyone's name the way you screamed mine? I can make you come like that again. I can make you come so many times you won't even remember your own."

Her chest is rising and falling, fast and hard. She's staring fixedly at her hands and no doubt trying not to give in to me. She doesn't want to acknowledge those needs of hers. Perhaps she's afraid of what that makes her, and I want to teach her that it makes her a goddess. Just as mine makes me a god. We belong together, she and I. We always have.

"Coming is easy," she says, determinedly casual. "Anyone can do that."

"If that's the case, then why not say yes?" I ask. "But this is a one-night offer. You know who I am now. You know what I am. So, if you choose to walk out that door tonight, that's it. You're gone for good."

She flicks a glance up at me. "What do you mean?"

I stare back. "This is me, Katherine. I want what I want, and I won't compromise. But if this is truly not what you want, then you can leave. I won't stop you. You can't change your mind and come back, though. It's now or never, sweet girl."

Giving a time limit can be helpful for making decisions, though if she walks out now, I'll probably follow. Now she's here, I can't bear for her to leave.

Her eyes flare at the sound of my old pet name for her. "Tate, this is—"

"Too fast? You need more time?" I interrupt. "You know already what decision you're going to make. Your body has made it for you. It's just going to take a couple of moments for your mind to catch up."

"Oh, fuck you," she snaps, but there's a lack of heat in the words.

I smile. "You can certainly fuck me, but only if you earn the right to do so."

She snorts. "So, you want to have sex? That's basically what you're saying, right?"

"Essentially," I reply. "But this time we'll be doing it my way."

"Is there any other way but your way?"

She's being flippant, trying to minimize the tension, but I'm not going to let her. "You don't have to pretend," I say. "The Katherine I knew was braver than that."

A strange expression crosses her face, but it's gone before I have time pinpoint what it is. She looks away again, her jaw tight.

You can ask questions," I go on. "You can ask any question you like, and I'll answer honestly. None of this works without honesty."

She's silent a moment, then she finally asks, as if the words have been forced from her, "Okay, fine. So.... how *does* it all work?"

"It works like this. You give me your total submission,

33

which means submitting to me in every way, both mentally and physically, for the length of the scene." I pin her gaze with mine, so she understands. "Submission is a gift. It's an exercise in trust. As a Dom, I have to keep that trust, that gift, safe. And in return, I will take control of your body and your mind, and I will give you pleasure beyond anything you've ever experienced."

She blinks but doesn't look away.

"But I get nothing if you don't give me your submission first," I continue. "It's a power exchange. You get to give up control for however long you want, which means you don't have to do anything, you don't have to make any decisions, and you let me do all the work. And I get to take that control. I get to dominate you, while keeping you and your trust safe, and that gives me enormous pleasure." I pause. "But again, if you don't give me that gift, I don't get a fucking thing."

"But you could just take it, couldn't you?" she asks, her expression guarded.

Instantly, I'm on high alert. It's a valid question, but now I'm wondering if she had an experience with a Dom that wasn't good. It would explain her fear and her reluctance to admit that she's submissive.

"No," I say flatly, making sure she understands. "It's not submission if it's taken by force, and that's not what I'm into. I want the gift, Katherine. And I want you to give it to me willingly." I stare at her. "Did that happen to you? Did someone take it by force?"

She doesn't answer, leaning back on the couch, her hands still clasped, self-possessed and self-contained, not giving me a single fucking thing. It's infuriating, and she probably knows that.

"When I imagined meeting you again, I didn't think that

this would be the kind of discussion we'd have," she says at last.

I want to push and keep pushing until I get the truth from her, but she's not there yet. I need to be patient, so I only smile. "What other discussion would we have here? In a sex club?"

"True."

"It's just a night, Katherine," I say. "It doesn't have to mean anything you don't want it to."

Except it will, of course.

It will mean everything, and I will make sure of it.

5

Lucas

I stand at the back of the crowd by a column, keeping half an eye on the newbies while the other half is constantly drawn to the alcove where Tate and Katherine are sitting.

Fuck, I can still feel the shock of seeing her echoing through me.

I'd felt someone staring at me from the bar area, so I'd looked, and there was Katherine, sitting on a barstool, staring back, just as shocked to see me as I was to see her.

It hit me then, like a fucking crowbar to the back of the head, that toxic mix of desire and fury and guilt that I always felt around her. It filled my veins, made my blood pump hard, and my breath catch.

My fucking breath doesn't catch for anyone.

I thought it was behind me, I thought I was done with it, but apparently my body didn't get the fucking memo, and I'm so fucking furious I want to punch a wall.

She tried to run when she saw me, but instead of heading out the door like she should have, she turned and went deeper into the club. And like the goddamn stupid bastard I am, I followed. I had to tell Tate she was here — at least that was the plan. Until she ran into him.

I knew he wasn't going to let her go the instant he saw her. He never lets go of anything he considers his, and I'm the same. We're possessive motherfuckers.

Jesus, it should be over, this damn pull I feel inside whenever she's around. Like she put her hand around my cock, and I can't help but follow her wherever she wants to go.

She's beautiful, still. Bright red hair, pale skin, and her eyes the same shade of blue as the Montana sky, where I used to live with the one foster family I ever liked. And she was as good a friend to me as she was to Tate. A sweet girl, that's what he used to call her, and she was.

I used to call her Katie, though.

I glower at the newbies clustered around the stage. Some woman is inching closer, getting far too caught up in what's happening on stage, and putting her hands on the edge. If she gets any nearer, I'll have to intervene.

My jaw tightens, tension creeping through me, and I stretch my neck from one side to the other to release it. Just knowing that Katie is in the same room is affecting me way more than it should, and I need to get it the fuck together.

Tate's always known my feelings about her, though we never talk about it. Just as he knows I'd never take her from him — not that he'd let me anyway. He saw her first, and it is what it is. It's my shit to handle, and he trusts me to handle it.

I was young when he and I met her — too young — and I didn't know how to deal with my feelings for her. She and Tate had such a volatile relationship, and I found myself in the role of mediator more often than I was comfortable with. She turned to me a lot when things got bad with Tate, and I was idiot enough to offer her a shoulder to cry on. Idiot because we had a shitload of physical chemistry and I couldn't resist her. She was warm, bright, and funny, and she was the first person other than Tate who actually seemed to care about me.

I'm older now, though, and like Tate, I know myself better. My feelings for her are what they are, and I'll keep my anger and guilt to myself. Channel them in my preferred way, such as finding myself a nice little sub for the night. Tate fucked Cherry into insensibility just before, but once she's recovered, I'm sure she'll be up for more. She's a greedy little thing, and she knows what I like. A sweet, obedient girl who only wants to please.

I shift on my feet, surveying the crowd by the stage yet again to make sure they're behaving themselves. Katie's friend is near the front. She's totally hooked by the action, not missing Katie at all, which is good. A guy off to one side is leaning forward and looking up at Nell as if he's seen God. Nell can handle herself, naturally, but it's my job as a monitor to make sure the rules of the club are obeyed. Especially the 'no touching' rule.

He puts out a hand, and instantly I'm moving, making my way through the crowd, gently easing people out of my way until I get to the front of the stage.

"No touching," I growl at the guy with way more temper than I should since it's newbies night and mistakes are going to be made. But I lost all my patience the moment Katie walked in, along with the remains of my good mood. "Do that again and you're out."

The guy glances at me, but I stare him down until he finally mutters an apology and steps back from the stage. I nod, take a look once more at the crowd to make sure everyone is behaving themselves, then go back to my post.

Once there, I glance again at the alcove where Tate and Katie are, making sure no one's disturbing them. Regardless of my personal feelings, I know this is important shit for Tate right now. He always meant to find her, and it seems like fate that she turned up here tonight. I don't want anything to jeopardize that. Tate's the brother I never had, and I'm that for him, and we have each other's backs. It's always been that way.

Yet I can't resist glancing at her. She's sitting on the couch, her hands clasped in her lap, looking down at them. Even from here, I can see the tender, pale skin at her nape, and I want to put my hand there. Grip her gently like a cat with a kitten and have her relax back against me.

She's not relaxed now, however. I can see the hunch in her shoulders. Understandable given the shock it must have been to not only see me, but Tate too.

Ten fucking years it's been, and there she is, her fire-red hair in a tidy bun, all dressed up in a suit. She always seemed to me to be like a dahlia in full bloom, but now she looks as if life has crumpled her petals.

Fuck. I need to stop looking at her.

I pull my gaze away, but nothing can stop my thoughts from going over and over our relationship from years ago. Late-night talks on the phone when she and Tate were arguing. Hugs when she was upset since Tate wasn't physically demonstrative. Talking about books, since she and I had that in common.

And then, that night before she walked out, her turning up at my front door, crying because she'd had a terrible argument with Tate. She wouldn't tell me what it was about, but the hug I gave her had ended with a kiss, and her running out on me, too. She left the next day.

I didn't tell Tate that we'd kissed. It would have served no purpose, so I kept it to myself. But I don't doubt that her feelings for me were another reason she fled from Tate, and the guilt from that ate me up inside.

I fold my arms and lean back against the column again. On stage, Nell is using a flogger on Amy and is explaining its use as she goes. Many of the crowd are wincing as the blows land, but there are more than a few who are looking a little flushed. There'll be plenty more signups to the app after this, I'm guessing.

"You okay?"

Tate's voice from beside me takes me by surprise, but I don't turn. "Is that a trick question?" I don't even attempt to mask the temper in my voice. He knows I'm pissed anyway.

He's silent for a moment, then asks, "Are we going to have a problem?"

I shift my shoulders against the column. "No. I handle my shit, you know that."

"Okay," he says. "I'm giving Katherine time."

I don't need to ask what he means. I know. He'll have laid it all out for her. Told her who and what he is, and what he wants. Now, she has to decide if that's what she wants, too.

"You think she's into it?" I ask, meaning the submissive part of it.

"Yes." I can hear the certainty in his voice, and it sends an uncomfortable bolt of heat through me. The thought of her kneeling for me is all too fucking clear, and it shouldn't be in my fucking head.

"But she's also afraid of it," he goes on. "And doesn't want to admit to anything."

I glance at him. "She was afraid ten years ago, too," I point out, keeping my tone neutral. We had words about it after she left because it was clear that, regardless of how she felt about me, she was mainly afraid of Tate's controlling nature. I'd seen the fear in her then, and had warned him about it, but he hadn't listened.

He blamed himself for it later, of course, which is why I don't want to heap more guilt onto him about it now. Still, if she's afraid, then care needs to be taken or he'll lose her again.

He scowls. "I'm not the same man I was ten years ago, Luc, you know that. I'm not going to force anything on her."

I sigh. "I didn't mean it like that. All I'm saying is don't push her too hard, too soon. You don't want to make her run again." And he has the potential to do that. He's a great Dom, but this isn't about just any sub. This is about Katie.

His expression hardens, and he looks toward the stage. He hates being told what to do — obviously — but he'll take it from me, even when I'm telling him something he doesn't want to hear.

For a moment or two, he's silent, watching Nell perform. Then he says, "No, I don't."

"Take it slow then," I say. "If this is all new to her, then keep the introduction simple."

Tate doesn't need my advice, not when he knows what to do already, but again, this is important, and he wants to hear what I have to say. Our skills as Doms lie in different directions, yet they complement each other. I'm a stickler for rules, as is he, but I like working with a sub's emotions, while he prefers mind games. We both like doling out punishments, but I am sparing with mine. Praise is more pleasurable for me — building a sub up is my forte, rather than breaking them. I also like aftercare, which he does not, and I prefer to be called Daddy rather than Sir.

I did once try being a switch, but I soon realized after a few scenes that submission isn't for me. I like control too much. Still, the experience has given me a good insight into what it's like for the sub, and I use that in my scenes.

Tate and I double-team a sub quite often, and that's the best rush. He and I work instinctively with each other, using our different strengths, and sometimes during a scene, it feels as if we're reading each other's minds. As if we're perfectly in sync, working together to bring the most pleasure to the sub.

He gives a nod to indicate he's heard, keeping his gaze on the stage. "I shouldn't have waited so long to find her," he says after a moment.

That was a discussion we'd had more than once. In the early days, it was too soon, then we started the company, and it got too busy. I was the one who told him to hold off, and yeah, part of that was not wanting her to come back into our lives again and screwing shit up again. The shit being me.

But Tate knew that.

"We were busy," I say. "The time wasn't right."

"You think it is now?"

"Why else would she be here?"

He glances at me and smiles, and it's ferocious. "That's what I told her."

There's a fire in him tonight, I can see it burn. A fire he's kept banked for years but left still smoldering. It's for her, that fire, and I'm glad to see it, because after she left, he got a little darker and a little angrier, and he stayed that way.

Getting involved with the BDSM scene helped. But his mom died young, and he had a shitty father, and a shitty upbringing, and he deserves to be happy.

He deserves to have her.

"So, what's she doing now?" I ask, after a moment, unable to resist.

"We didn't get into that," Tate says. "From the looks of that suit she's wearing, I'd say she's working in a law firm."

I'm not surprised. That's always what she'd wanted, and she was determined to get there.

"That's it?" I ask. "You didn't ask her any questions about her life at all?"

"No," Tate says, not looking chastened about it one bit. "We can talk about that later."

Despite my foul temper, I almost want to laugh. Typical Tate. He's too fucking impatient, that's his problem. "Christ," I murmur. "You really know how to seduce a woman."

"Some women don't need to be seduced." He's still looking at the stage, a smile playing around his mouth. "Some women are already there."

Instinctively, I glance over to the alcove again, to check on Katie, to make sure she hasn't run off, and this time she's got her head up, looking in our direction. Her gaze meets mine, and like it did when she first came in, I feel the impact of it. She goes very still, and I don't look away, allowing my authority to bleed through as I test the arcing chemistry between us.

It's still there, still strong, I can feel it. But fuck, you'd think I'd have learned by now. Testing our chemistry all those years ago only added to her fear, and it's probably doing the same thing now. I can't be responsible for her running out on Tate a second time, I just can't.

"I need a favor," Tate says.

I drag my attention back to him. "Sure. What do you need?"

He glances at me. "I want her to watch a scene, so she knows what she's getting into. You up for that?"

A curl of heat wraps itself around my cock at the thought of doing a scene with Katie watching. Yet part of me is still fucking pissed, and Tate asking for this, especially knowing how I feel about her, is shitty.

"What?" I raise a brow. "Like baby's first Dom?"

Tate's green eyes narrow. "Put it the fuck away, Luc," he says flatly, ignoring my barb and addressing the real reason for my bad temper, the sharp, fucking asshole. "I'm asking you because I trust you. You know the rules, and I know you'll show her what she needs to see."

I let out a breath, take a leisurely survey of the crowd, and try to get my foul mood under control. Again, this is not his problem. It's mine, and it's up to me to handle it, and if I'm not careful, I'll turn this into a bigger deal than it needs to be.

"Yeah, okay," I say at last, glancing back at him. "I was going to find Cherry to relieve a little tension, anyway. You want to do this now?"

He nods. "Nothing like striking while the iron is hot."

"Give me fifteen then."

Tate gazes at me for a moment. "Thanks, Luc," he says, and I know what the thanks is really for.

"It's okay." I meet his stare with one of my own. "But don't let her get away again. If I have to go through more years of your emotional bullshit, I'm going to move to fucking France."

He gives me another of his ferocious smiles. "Oh, don't you worry. The Eiffel Tower can wait. I'm not letting her leave here without me."

6

Katherine

I'm sitting on the couch, my mouth dry. I'd just gotten myself together after Tate went off to let me think about things, and I was looking in his direction, only to meet Lucas's gaze staring back. And like a witness under an excellent cross-examination, all my poise crumbled away beneath the weight of that gaze. It was knowing, authoritative, and crackling with an electricity that made static crawl all over my skin.

I couldn't look away, and neither did he, memories of how he kissed me the night before I left filling the space between us.

I'd had a confrontation with Tate that night. He'd accused me of being distant with him and how it felt as if I was pulling away, and he wanted me to tell him what the issue was. But I didn't want to talk about it, because I didn't want to get into having to explain the assault with him. Anyway, in the end, Tate had banged out of the house, disappearing into the night, and after waiting for hours for him to come home, I'd gone to Lucas's to see if he was there. He wasn't, but I'd ended up weeping on Lucas, which had then ended up with him kissing me, and that was my final straw.

I had to leave. I had to get away from the growing distance between Tate and me, and my confusing feelings for Lucas, too, so I did.

I look down at my hands, trying yet again to get myself together, thinking about what Tate said, about who he is now, and what he wants. I bet he's a terrifying Dom, but thank God I'm not submissive, no matter what he says about me obeying him. Bringing up our sex life was unfair, though, the bastard. Especially the times when he restrained me, though I'd rather forget that.

Still, he's not wrong. Sex was at the root of our issues. I was emotionally distant with him because I wanted to forget the whole assault thing, but he demanded total honesty, and I couldn't give it.

And it *was* an assault. I know that intellectually. He gave me no choice about it, and I know that my mother calling me a little slut afterwards was toxic. But my feelings of shame then got all tangled up with Tate and his need for control in the bedroom, and it was impossible for me back then to untangle them.

Now, though, it's different. I left that confused little girl behind me when I got my law degree and moved from California to New York, and now sex isn't the big deal that it used to be. I mean, I have it, and it's fine. I'm in control of it, and that's how I like it to be. It's not confusing. It's straightforward and easy and uncomplicated, and I prefer it that way.

However, I can't stop thinking about Tate and what he said about how submitting to him is a gift. How he'll keep my trust safe, and that it's a power exchange. That he'll do all the work, and what I receive in return is pleasure beyond anything I've ever experienced.

Regardless of how confused my feelings about him were back then, one thing was for sure. Tate O'Rourke was one hell of a thrill ride. He was passionate, ferociously intelligent, intensely exciting, and he made me feel as if I were the only woman in the world worth looking at, or talking to. Everything seemed more interesting and exciting when he was around, and he was just as ambitious for me as he was for himself. He never thought my dreams of being a lawyer were stupid, and he wanted me to go for them.

So now those old feelings I used to have for him are churning away inside me. They haven't gone. And he's probably counting on them to make me stay, and part of me wants to do that to prove I *don't* still feel the same way, that he means nothing and whatever kink he wants to show me means nothing, either.

You're curious, though. Don't deny it.

Of course, I deny it. I'm not curious in the least, and definitely not about submission.

The air around me shifts, like a change in pressure, and I look up to find Tate standing there, his gaze on mine. A jolt goes through me, hot and electric, and I'm acutely aware of our height difference, with me sitting while he's standing, towering over me like a giant redwood.

I'm not afraid, though, and that other feeling inside me is *not* excitement. It can't be. I'm over him.

"I haven't made any dec—" I begin.

"I want to show you something," he interrupts before I can finish my sentence. "I've organized a scene for you, so that you can watch and see how it's done."

Another electric jolt goes through me. I haven't been watching what's happening on the stage, but from the one or two glimpses I've had, it looks like a live sex show. Which there would be given that this is a sex club, as Tate so eloquently pointed out. That's what you do in clubs like these, right? You watch sex happening in front of you, and while it's not for me, it's no big deal.

"You want me to watch people have sex?" I ask, mainly for extra clarification, since that's indeed what it sounds like.

His green gaze flicks over my face, studying me. "Yes. I want you to see the interaction, see how good it feels for the sub and the Dom, too."

My pussy, the traitorous bitch, throbs, while my heartbeat accelerates. I ignore both of them, trying to remain cool. The way Tate watches me makes heat start to burn deep inside, my skin pulling tight. He used to do that when we were together, watching me like a hawk with a rabbit, and it made me breathless, made me want him. It's aggravating that it still does.

I should get up and leave, that's what I should do, not sit here letting him dictate everything, but even if I had an excuse ready, he'd take that as an acknowledgement that he's getting to me, and I don't want that.

"I don't know," I say, prevaricating. "I'm not really into voyeurism."

"You won't be in the room," Tate says. "You'll be watching through a window. They won't see you."

"They? You mean, you're not going to do...uh...the scene?" The word 'scene' feels awkward on my tongue, like a different language.

He smiles, as if I've said something endearing. "No. I'm not taking part."

Something trips inside me, and I can't work out whether it's relief or disappointment.

Yet before I have a chance to sort through that or even speak, he's holding out a peremptory hand to me. "Come, Katherine," he orders, his voice deep and authoritative. "I don't want to waste yet more of the night with indecision."

And once again, like I found myself sitting when he told me to, I find myself rising to my feet and putting my hand in his, before my brain even engages. His long fingers close around mine, the warmth of his skin sending prickles of heat through me.

Fuck's sake, I can't believe I stood when he told me to and took his hand. I can't believe I obeyed, just like that. I don't like it. I don't like how it's an instinctive thing, how my body obeys him, even though my brain is very unhappy about it.

I know I could pull my hand out of his, but that would acknowledge that all of this is a problem, and it's not. And while I shouldn't care what he thinks of me, I care enough that I don't want to give him the satisfaction of looking like a coward. He told me I used to be brave, and maybe that's affected me more than I want to admit.

Anyway, Jesus, why am I overthinking this? It's only sex. It's not life or death.

So, I don't protest, allowing him to lead me to a curtained doorway at the back of the club, and I follow as he pulls aside the curtain and we step into a dim hall lined with doors, all closed. There are small windows in each door, and as we go past a couple of them, there are larger windows that look out into the hall, too, giving a good view into the room beyond.

I catch glimpses of a four-poster bed in one room, nothing at all in another, before we stop outside the window into a third.

The room is simple, a giant bed pushed up against one wall, an armchair in the corner, and a chest of drawers opposite the bed. It's as dimly lit as the hallway, and I feel as if I'm at the zoo, in the darkness of the nocturnal house, watching the animals who only come out at night.

A shiver passes through me, a strange kind of anticipation gathering in my gut. Tate's fingers have mine in a strong grip, and I half wonder if I were to pull away, would he let me go? It doesn't feel as if he would, which makes an unwanted thread of excitement curl through me, and instantly I want to pull away. But that would be stupid, and again, admitting all of this affects me, and it doesn't.

I'm wondering how long I have to stand here watching this empty room when a door at the back opens, and a woman walks in. She's completely naked and apparently cool with that, because she gives the window a flirty little wave, acknowledging us, and I hear Tate mutter something under his breath.

Then she turns her back to us, and a man walks into the room after her.

And all the air rushes out of my lungs, because it's Lucas.

Really? I'm going to watch fucking Lucas have sex?

A low throb of heat pulses through me, betraying me, but I force it away.

What I felt once for him is gone, along with what I felt for Tate. Neither of them affects me anymore, and I'm definitely *not* turned on by the thought of watching him fuck some woman. Especially not with Tate also watching.

I say nothing, trying not to tense. I don't want to give away to Tate that I'm bothered by Lucas's presence in any way. But then he says, almost soothingly, "Luc is only going to show you what it's all about. He's an excellent Dom who knows what he's doing. With a little help from Cherry, of course."

"Sure," I say, trying to be casual, but my voice is husky. "I guess I shouldn't be surprised he's a Dom, too."

"Oh, he tried being a switch, but it didn't take."

"A switch?" I'll probably regret asking this.

"Enjoys being both a Dominant and submissive."

Lucas as a submissive? I can't see it. Not even a little bit. There was no mistaking the look he gave me out there, full of authority and will.

Fucking hot.

No. No, not at all.

"I'm not surprised," I say, again trying to be casual and unaffected

"No," Tate says, moving a little closer. "But that experience makes him an excellent Dom, since he knows what it's like to be a sub."

Lucas is dressed a little more formally now than he was

out in front of the stage. He's wearing a waistcoat and jacket over his white shirt, though he's not wearing a tie. He looks...phenomenal. I don't want to admit it, but he does.

He does not give us a wave. He doesn't even look at the window. Instead, his attention is all on Cherry. He says something to her — the room must be soundproofed because I can't hear what he says — and she turns her back to him, her gaze on the floor.

Lucas moves over to the chest of drawers, and then he gets something out of one of the drawers. A pair of black leather, padded handcuffs, joined by a very short chain.

Something inside me clenches tight, but again I ignore it. They're just a pair of handcuffs, and I've seen those before.

Lucas takes the cuffs over to where Cherry is standing and issues another order. She puts her hands behind her back, and he calmly puts the handcuffs on her, securing her wrists together at the base of her spine. Then he says something else, and she turns around to face him. Her head is lowered.

I'd forgotten how tall Lucas is. He's of a height with Tate, making Cherry look petite as she stands in front of him. He puts a finger beneath her chin and tilts her face up, his gaze meeting hers. And I feel the charge between them at the eye contact. It crackles outwards to where I'm standing, prickling over my skin and making goosebumps rise everywhere.

I know what it's like to meet his gaze, how it gets under your skin, and for one mad minute, I imagine myself standing there in front of him, and he's tilting my face up to look into my eyes.

But no, I can't think like that, I can't *ever* think like that. He was hot back then, and he's even hotter now, but he's Tate's friend and I'm not getting all tangled up in that again.

Except I can't stop looking at him as he gazes down at Cherry. The lines of his fallen-angel face are hard, the authority radiating from him palpable. Even in the dim lighting, I can see the threads of gold in his hair. And no matter how hard I pretend I'm unaffected, a small part of me shakes, my heartbeat sounding loud in my ears.

Lucas points to a spot on the floor, and Cherry moves over to it, and kneels.

"You see how she's kneeling for him?" Tate murmurs, sounding even closer. "She's given him the control, and now it's his job to make her feel good. She doesn't have to do a thing. The cuffs are for her pleasure, because she likes restraints."

I want to say 'how nice for her' but I'm suddenly aware of Tate's aftershave. It's dark, masculine, bergamot, and something else, like cedar, and I find myself wondering what it is, because it's delicious. Ten years ago, he used to smell of engine oil, sun, and clean male sweat, and I loved it just as much.

In the room beyond, Lucas is shrugging out of his jacket and laying it carefully on the bed. Then he undoes his cuffs one by one, rolling up his sleeves to expose his muscled forearms. Every movement unhurried and precise, and almost unbearably sexy. There are stars tattooed the length of one forearm, and a dark mandala on the other, with flowers woven into it, and it flows down his wrist and onto the back of his hand. It's beautiful.

Those tattoos are new. He didn't have them ten years ago, at least, and I wish I felt nothing at all about them, about him. I wish I didn't think they were beautiful, that he was beautiful, and most especially, I wish there wasn't this heat that's burning inside me now.

"You can ask questions." Tate's deep voice is soft and close. "You can ask me anything you like."

I swallow yet again, trying to get some moisture into my dry mouth, attempting once more to be cool and in control. "Why is she kneeling?" It's the first question that comes into my head.

"Because he told her to. She doesn't have to do anything or think about anything. All she has to do is obey him."

"Seems wrong," I say, even as I'm aware of a growing pressure between my thighs.

Tate only laughs, soft and deep, and knowing. It makes my face heat, and I hope desperately that he can't see it. I don't want him to know that this is affecting me in any way.

Lucas goes over to where Cherry is kneeling and looks down at her. His hands move to his belt, and he slowly unbuckles it. They're side on to the window, so I can see her face, and while her attention is on the floor, her whole body is quivering.

"If you're wondering, she's not trembling because she's afraid," Tate says, his voice sounding even closer. "She's just extremely turned on right now."

I'm not wondering. I know she's turned on, because I can feel the same quiver inside me. I want to fight it. Push it away somehow. It reminds me of things I'd rather stay forgotten.

Lucas unbuttons his pants and pulls the zipper down, and everything in me draws tight. Oh, God. Does he know that I'm watching him right now? That I'm right here on the other side of this window? But of course, he does. Tate must have asked him to give me a demonstration, and that's why he's not looking our way. He must hate this, surely.

But you don't.

I want to. I really, really want to. I want to turn and walk

JACKIE ASHENDEN

back through the doorway and get out of this club. Feel the humid, summer night air on my face, instead of watching Lucas Thorne.

But I can't bring myself to move as he reaches down and pulls his cock out, and I go still. It's long, thick, and very hard, and the way he's holding it, gripping it in his large, tattooed fist, is so incredibly sexy I can't breathe.

Years ago, when I'd first met Tate and Lucas, and it was the three of us against the world, I used to have dirty fantasies about both of them. I was seeing Tate at the time, but I couldn't stop thinking about Lucas. Couldn't stop thinking about what it might be like to do the same things Tate and I did, but with him.

It was wrong then, and it's wrong now, but still, my heartbeat is so loud I'm sure Tate will hear it, so I try to school my expression. Make it as blank as I can. To not let on in any way that Lucas is turning me on.

He gives another order, and Cherry comes into an upright kneeling position, lifting her head and opening her mouth. He guides his cock between her lips, all his attention is on her, and he says something, making her gaze lift. Again, I feel that charge, their eye contact electric. Then he pushes his hands into her hair and grips it tight, using it to guide her head as he begins to thrust into her mouth.

My face is on fire. I can't believe I'm still watching. No matter how many times I tell myself it's just sex, no big deal, I'm increasingly unable to ignore the throb between my legs. I'm also conscious of the cotton of my bra pressing against my hardening nipples and no amount of thinking it's just the temperature makes any difference. Because it's not the temperature, and I know that.

Cherry's mouth is stretched wide around Lucas's cock, and his hands in her hair must hurt. He's pushing deeper,

56

yet keeping his thrusts slow and deliberate, as if he's coaxing her to take more of him, and I can't stop staring at her face. At the way she's looking up at him, eyes wide, as if he's God himself.

I know how Tate tasted. He used to love it when I took him in my mouth. But now I'm helplessly wondering how Lucas tastes. Would he look at me the way he's looking at Cherry? Would I look at him the way she's looking at him?

"Do you remember doing this with me?" Tate murmurs in my ear. He's not beside me now, but behind me. I can feel the heat of his body against my back, the scent of him all around me. "I remember," he goes on, his voice almost hypnotic. "You had the hottest mouth. I could have fucked it forever."

A shiver passes over my skin. I do remember. He taught me how to do it and showed me exactly what he liked. He preferred me like Cherry, on my knees at his feet, but I didn't like kneeling for him. It felt subservient and humiliating, but the worst part was how much it turned me on.

Abruptly, Lucas pulls out of Cherry's mouth. He's still hard, but he tucks himself away as if he isn't. She's looking up at him, and if I'm not much mistaken, the expression on her face is a pleading one. He shakes his head, and she says something in return, making him crouch down in front of her. He takes her chin in his hand, still making that electric eye contact, and he's telling her something that makes her tremble.

I'm trembling too, and if I'm not careful, it's going to become next to impossible to hide. Tate feels like a giant at my back, his dark presence surrounding me. He's not touching me, and yet I'm acutely conscious of him.

You want him to push you up against the wall.

No, fuck no. I don't want that. I spent so long trying to

forget how that one experience warped my sexuality forever, and I really don't want all this bullshit with Tate to remind me.

In the room beyond the window, Lucas rises to his feet, issuing an order and pointing to the bed. Cherry gets to her feet, too, with surprising grace, given she has her hands handcuffed behind her. She moves over to the bed and sits on the end, wriggling up on the mattress and lying back. Lucas goes to the chest of drawers again and gets more cuffs out, taking them back to the bed. Then he fastens them around each of her ankles, before attaching them to special rings at each corner of the bed frame, so she's lying with her legs spread wide, unable to close them.

She's open to him, available in every way, with her hands locked behind her. Her nipples are hard, and she's breathing very fast; I can see the rise and fall of her chest.

"She's at his mercy," Tate murmurs in my ear, reading my mind. "Completely and totally. And she loves it."

Does she, though? There's no choice to be had in any of this, not for her.

You like it. You always have.

I ignore the thought as Lucas comes to stand at the end of the bed, looking down between her spread legs. Then he puts his hands on her thighs, gripping them tightly, and he bends down, putting the flat of his tongue on her pussy, licking her like an ice cream cone.

She jerks on the bed, her back arching at the contact, her mouth open in a cry, and this I can't hide the sound of my own breath catching. The pulse between my thighs gets more and more insistent, my cotton panties damp and getting damper.

"That could be you," Tate goes on in that dark voice. "Cuffed and spreadeagled for me. Unable to move. If you were very good, I'd eat your pussy until you screamed, and if you weren't, I'd toy with it until you're so desperate to come, you'd do anything for me."

I want to tell him to shut the hell up, that I don't want to be at his mercy, or anyone's mercy, not again. I don't want to feel as if my pleasure is being forced from me without my consent, no matter how much my body might enjoy that. It's always been a liar.

Lucas's head is between Cherry's legs, his tongue lapping at her, licking the folds of her pussy. She's quivering like a tree in a storm, her eyes closed. He pauses and says something, and her eyes open. She looks down at him, and he looks back, licking and nipping, eating her as if she's his finest meal.

I feel as if it's his tongue between my legs, as if I could come just by thinking about it, and I don't know how I got to this point, or why I can't resist, but I can't keep watching anymore. Any minute now, Tate's going to know just how turned on I am, and I can't bear the thought of that.

I start to turn away, but that's when I feel Tate's large, warm hand take my jaw in his palm, and he turns my head firmly back to the window. He has me in a tight grip, making it impossible for me to move. "Watch," he orders, low and dark in my ear, his breath warm against my skin. "Watch her come. I want you to see her face when she does, because what she's feeling is incredible."

I freeze, everything in me going still. I remember how searing his touch was, how my skin would go tight and hot at the merest brush of his fingers. In bed, he was a fire I tried to control, yet only ended up being consumed by, and I feel that same way now as his hand holds my jaw. Yet that dirtiness, that shame is also there too, memories of that guy's irresistible strength as he pushed me against the wall and held me there flooding through me. How I didn't want it and yet liked it at the same time, and how confusing that was.

"If you don't want this," Tate says quietly. "Say 'red,' and I'll let you go."

A little shock winds through the heat building inside me. I don't know how he's picked up on my tension, but he has, and it's weird, because he never used to be that observant.

I don't know what to do now. I don't want to keep watching. I don't want this rapidly building desire or the complicated feelings that come with it. But he's given me an out, and a part of me wants to take it. Because who cares if he knows I can't handle this? He told me his offer was a one-night thing, so if I walk away, I'll never have to see him or Lucas again.

Yet, I don't want to be a coward, either. Ten years ago, I ran away from both of them because I was afraid, and I always believed that I left that girl behind me. But I won't have left her behind if I say 'red'. I'll have given in to it instead.

So, I give my head a brief shake to let him know I won't be saying anything, let alone 'red', and keep watching as Cherry's face flushes, her expression becoming desperate as she stares at Lucas between her thighs. I can see her mouth move, but he's shaking his head.

"She's only going to come when he says," Tate murmurs. "He's in control, and she can't come unless he permits it."

I can't quite hide how I'm trembling, and all I can think about is the feel of Tate's fingers pressed against my skin. His touch is so hot, like little flames burning me.

"That seems unlikely," I force out, hating how husky my voice is, because it betrays me too much.

Tate gives a soft laugh. "Oh, she will." He's so certain.

"Luc will make sure of that. That's his job." His thumb moves on the underside of my jaw, lightly stroking, and sparks crackle over my skin. Everywhere. "I can make you do that, too."

I'm shivering and I can't stop. "No. N-no, you can't."

"Oh, sweet girl." His lips brush the side of my neck, and I shiver even harder. "There's no end to the things I can make you do."

7

Tate

I can feel the quiver of her body through my fingers on her jaw. Her skin is as soft and warm as I remember. She was the one bright thing in my life, the only bright thing. Losing her was like losing the part of myself that still had hope of happiness in this fucked-up world, and I'm not letting that happen again.

Take it slow, Lucas said to me, and he wasn't wrong. He

never is, not when it comes to subs, so that's why I asked him for that favor. It was a shitty thing to ask, I knew that, especially given his feelings about her. But he was the best Dom for the job, and I trusted him to show her what she needed to know.

She can trust me as well. That's why I gave her a safe word, because I could feel her tension and her resistance, and I needed her to know she has an out if things get too much.

But there's something about being aroused that scares her, and I want to know what the fuck it is. She was scared ten years ago, and she still is, and I'm tired of her secrets. I need to know if it's me, if I'm the one who frightened her back when we were together, because if so, I need to fix it.

She didn't say the word, though. She just shook her head, and I had second thoughts about continuing, because if she's white knuckling her way through this, then she needs to fucking stop. But she was aroused, I knew it. I could smell it. And I suspect — though she'd never admit it — she was getting off on watching Lucas. Another thing she could never hide from me.

She wanted him the way he wanted her, and I was aware of it even back then. It used to drive me crazy the way she looked at him, but I never said anything to her, because I knew neither of them would cross any lines. They're too loyal. I also knew that Lucas gave her something she couldn't get from me, and that if he hadn't, she would have left me long before she actually did.

Apparently, she still feels the same about him, because I could see it in her face the moment he walked into the room. Her eyes went wide, and her whole body stiffened, and her attention has been glued to him ever since. Watching him undo his cuffs and roll up his sleeves.

Watching him take his cock out. Watching him eat Cherry out.

The scent of her arousal is in the air, a sweet musk mixing with the lavender body wash she used to use. Seems she still does, and now I'm hard as a rock, the smell of her so familiar to me, even after all these years.

I want to push things, so I ease her against the glass of the window, pinning her there with my body. "You want to say 'red'?" I ask, checking in on her.

She's trembling and makes a soft sound, but it's not 'red', so I stroke the underside of her jaw, making sure her attention stays on the action beyond the glass.

Lucas is working Cherry into a frenzy, her legs pulling against the cuffs as she lifts her hips to his mouth. Little brat is trying to get her orgasm before she's allowed, probably wanting to earn a punishment. She's quite the pain slut that one, but I don't think Lucas will punish her with a crop or a flogger, not for this particular demonstration. Not with Katherine watching.

He'll punish her in a different way, and I can see he's already doing that, lifting his mouth from between her legs before she's ready, leaving her trembling on the bed.

I'm a little surprised when he undoes his pants for the second time, taking his time as he leisurely gets out his cock, takes a condom packet from his pocket, opens it, and rolls the latex down. He likes to fuck a sub in a scene, though he usually makes them wait far longer than this. Clearly, he's impatient, though he's making a whole production of it now. Cherry is into it, her gaze pinned to his every move.

Katherine is still tense, though — I can feel the resistance in her jaw. But she's not saying 'red', and while not saying it when she should is a punishable offence, I can't bring myself to let her go. Sometimes a sub needs to be pushed out of their comfort zone, and I'm betting this applies to Katherine, too.

So, I keep hold of her, making her watch as Lucas pulls Cherry down to the end of the bed. He pushes into her, going slowly, making her writhe on the mattress, her mouth open. We can't hear her, but I know she'll be wailing like she did on stage when I was fucking her.

"Tate..." Katherine whispers. "I can't...I don't..."

I nuzzle against the side of her neck and am rewarded by her total body shiver. "It's okay to be turned on. That's the whole idea. But if you need to say 'red', then say it."

She jerks her head in negation again. Stubborn woman.

I press against her a little harder, intensifying the experience, pushing her. Again, I only get a soft gasp in response, so I stay there, letting her adjust to the sensation of my body against hers. The heat of me. The feel of me. Her ass is a delicious softness against my groin, and I want to grind my cock against her, make her beg and plead.

I tried to get her to submit years ago, before I knew what I was doing, and sometimes sex would feel like a battle, both of us fighting for supremacy. All I wanted was for her to give in, but she wouldn't. She was never as comfortable with her sexuality as I was, and it scared her. *I* scared her.

I want answers. I want to know why she was so afraid, why she couldn't talk about it, but most of all, I want to know why she left without a fucking word.

Lucas thinks I'm impatient, the fucker. I'm not, though, not when it comes to getting what I want. I've waited ten years for this, and what is that if not patience?

Cherry's mouth is moving and I know what's happening now. "He's making her beg for it," I say in Katherine's ear. "You'd beg, too, wouldn't you? If he had his cock inside you?"

She tries to shake her head, but once again she's lying. Her pretty face is nearly the same color as her hair, and her breathing is fast and uneven.

"What are you thinking about?" I place my free hand on her hip, even as I grip her jaw with the other. "Are you thinking about yourself lying on that bed? Are you thinking about Lucas's cock fucking you?"

Once again, she tries to shake her head, but her breathing is even faster now.

She knows she can say 'red' at any time, but she's also stubborn. The thing is that I'm stubborn too, and if she wants to be pushed, I'll push her. Hard.

"Little liar," I murmur, sliding my hand down over her thigh, finding the hem of her prim skirt, and pulling it up. "I think I'd better check for myself."

My fingers find her bare skin beneath the hem, soft as silk, and she shakes as I ease my hand between her thighs. She's wearing cotton panties, which is sweet, and they're wet, which is even sweeter. I expect some protest, but she only makes a soft sound as I brush the tips of my fingers over the fabric, her body jerking under my touch.

Oh yes, this is what I remember. Her responsiveness. She could never help herself when it came to me, and I won't lie, I used her desire shamelessly against her, especially when I felt the distance between us start to grow wider and wider.

It's intensely satisfying to feel the evidence of her hunger, to be certain that this is what she wants, even if her brain is taking a while to catch up with her body.

I press her more firmly against the glass. She's almost ready to come right here and now, I can tell from the way she's trembling and the quickened sound of her breathing.

Perhaps I should let her, give her a taste of how good her body can make her feel.

"Imagine yourself coming around Lucas's cock the way Cherry's about to," I breathe against the soft skin of her neck, pressing a finger down on her clit. "I can make you come with her."

Katherine shivers and gasps. I press harder, and she arches, the rounded curve of her ass pushing against my cock. She's panting, her frantic breath steaming the glass, and she's so wet she's soaked through the fabric of her panties.

"Watch," I order softly, brushing my mouth over her skin. "Watch her come, and then you'll come too."

She can't keep quiet now, a moan escaping her as I circle my finger, light strokes and gentle presses. Her body shudders as she moves her hips restlessly against my teasing fingertip. Fuck, she's so close.

In the room in front of us, I see Lucas finally give Cherry permission to come, and she's arching on the mattress, her mouth open in a soundless scream. At the same time, I press down on Katherine's clit, grinding her against the wall, using my body to keep her still, my mouth on her skin, and she gives an agonized cry as she comes, trembling and panting against me.

I keep her pressed against the wall as I take my hand away, holding her up as all the tension bleeds out of her and she jerks and shivers from the aftershocks.

Lucas gives Cherry a moment too, then pulls out of her. His jaw is tight, which means he's finding control difficult, and that's unusual for him. I'm surprised he's not letting himself come with her, because she's one of his favorites, but that's clearly not going to happen given the way he's rigidly tucking himself away. He sees to her restraints, unclipping the cuffs from her ankles, and then dealing with the ones around her wrists. After that's done, he scoops her up from the bed and carries her over to the armchair, sitting down with her, holding her in his arms.

"That's aftercare," I say softly, unable to resist brushing my lips over Katherine's skin yet again. "Lucas is better at it than I am."

She's still breathing fast, and I place my hands on the glass on either side of her, caging her against the wall while she gets her breath back.

Fuck, she smells so good. Familiar, warm. Like hope returning.

At least until she suddenly pushes back against me. "No, Tate," she says in a hoarse voice. "Give me some space."

I'm not at my best during aftercare. It's not my natural inclination, but this is Katherine, and even though we aren't in a scene, she needs some reassurance. I never provided that for her years ago, and I want to do it now, but there's a thin thread of panic in her voice, so I step back.

She doesn't move, and after a minute or two, her breathing slows.

"You okay?" I ask, shoving my hands into my pockets to keep from reaching for her. Fuck, did I push her too hard? I'll never forgive myself if I have, and neither will Lucas.

She's silent for a moment, then she lets out a breath. "Yes."

The word sounds firm, making me want to step closer again, to push and push and push, capitalize on that orgasm I gave her. But we're not in a scene, and I'm mindful of Lucas's warning, so I stay where I am.

She takes a breath, then eases back from the window, pulling her skirt back down and smoothing it with shaking hands, her back still toward me.

In the room beyond, Lucas strokes Cherry's hair, her head resting against his chest. But he's not looking down at her. This time, he's looking straight at the window, at us. No, at me. His gaze is direct, his jaw tight, and I know what that look means. He's put on a show for me, am I happy now?

As it happens, yes, fuck, given Katherine's reaction to it — to him, in fact — I'm not complaining. In fact, it's giving me an idea. First, though, I need to get her somewhere more private, where we can discuss things without distraction.

"Katherine," I say. "I think we need to talk."

8

Katherine

My hands are still shaking, and my legs feel weak. I'm barely able to hold myself upright. The aftershocks of the orgasm are still pulsing through me, and I just haven't got enough poise to turn and face him.

This is insane. I can't believe I couldn't resist. Not only did I let him push me up against the window, but I also let him touch me, too. Because watching Lucas with the sub in front of me, and then Tate's hot, hard body behind me, his scent so familiar, and the dirty things he was whispering in my ear.... God, I had no idea I liked dirty talk

I couldn't stop myself from imagining everything he said. Of me being on that bed, with Lucas inside me. Of me coming around his cock, the way the sub was about to. I should have pushed Tate away the way I used to when he was being bossy in bed, but.... I didn't.

I couldn't move, could only stand there, watching, as electric shivers from the warmth of Tate's breath and the brush of his mouth on my skin, with the slight prickle of his beard, crackled through me. Then he pushed me against the window, the pressure of his body pinning me there, and I got flashbacks of me at sixteen, when Mom's hookup held me against the wall and I was helpless to resist. How awful it was and yet, at the same time, how erotic. So confusing and wrong.

Then Tate put his hand under my skirt and touched me, and I came exactly when he wanted me to. I didn't have to work for it like I usually do — fuck, I was actually trying to resist it — but...he just touched me, and I was helpless before the intensity of it, blinded and crying out the way Cherry cried out.

Those same old feelings of shame had rushed through me, that not only did I not resist, but I let him do it to me in a public place. I let him get me off watching his best friend fuck some woman...

Maybe you're just a filthy slut, just like your mother said you were.

The thought is stuck in my head, and I can't get it out. I should have said 'red'. Tate told me to say it if I wanted things to stop, but I didn't, not even when he touched me.

You didn't want it to stop. That's the truth. You wanted every-thing he gave you.

I shut my eyes a moment as the thought echoes in my head, undeniable and unarguable. I didn't say 'red' because, no, I didn't want him to stop. I wanted him to touch me, and I wanted the pleasure only he has ever managed to give me.

Because that's the real truth. I don't want to be sexual, and I certainly don't want to be kinky, but that kind of blinding pleasure... God, I've never found it with anyone other than him. I've always had to work for my orgasms. Sometimes I can't even be bothered with them. But the one I just had came on so fast and so hard, there was nothing I could do to stop it.

Unable to face Tate quite yet, I open my eyes finally and stare through the glass at Lucas sitting in the armchair, holding Cherry in his arms instead. She's nestled against him, and his hand is moving idly in her hair, but he's not looking at her. His amber gaze is fierce as he focuses on the window, as if he's burning a hole through the glass.

He can't see me, but it doesn't matter. My cheeks are flaming anyway. He held me like that the night of my big blow-up with Tate, and I know how it feels to be in his arms with his hand stroking my hair...

"Katherine," Tate repeats, his deep voice making me shudder.

He knows how I got off on that, and no doubt he wants more.

You do too.

I close my eyes and take a breath. I don't. I shouldn't. I told myself I was vanilla all the way. But... maybe I'm not. Maybe I can't get this kind of pleasure from anyone else. I mean, I could find someone and tell them what I want, but that would involve a level of trust I've never given anyone.

And I know Tate. Sure, I find his ferocity and his authority scary, but he would never hurt me. It's funny. Even after ten years, I know I can trust him.

Submission is a gift...

It's only a night, that's what he said. And afterward, I can put both him and Lucas behind me. Definitely no talking, though, God forbid. Talking with Tate never leads anywhere good.

I collect myself and finally turn. He's standing behind me, tall and broad, his green gaze on mine, and I can feel the part of me that still wants him quiver with anticipation.

"No talking," I say coolly. "I think we've talked quite enough.

He raises one black brow. "Does that mean you're done for the evening?"

I swallow and then lift my chin. "It means if you want a night, you have it."

He is very still, but a spark in his eyes flickers then flares, like a match being struck. "Very well," he says, his voice neutral. "Come with me, then." He turns, and without looking back, walks down the dim hallway in the opposite direction to the club entrance.

I'm expecting him to gloat or even to show some kind of satisfaction at what he's made me give him, so his merely walking away is disconcerting. Especially when it's clear that I don't actually have to follow him if I don't want to, that he's giving me a choice about it, and for a minute I think about walking straight out of the club. But then he stops halfway down the hallway and turns. "Well?" he asks mildly.

No, I can't walk. If I want to exorcise some ghosts, then I need to commit. Test myself. The last time with Tate, I ran away, and I don't want to do that again. I'm not a fucking coward, not anymore.

So, I shrug and then follow him. He leads me down a bit further, to another door. There are no windows in this door, or windows into the hallway, which relieves me. I might be curious about the submissive kink stuff, but I'm not ready for other people watching me while I do it.

He takes a key out of his pocket and unlocks the door, then opens it for me, gesturing that I should go first.

"You a gentleman now?" I say dryly as I step inside the room.

"Oh no," Tate says, flashing me that smile of his. "Nothing gentlemanly about me."

I want to tell him there was certainly nothing gentlemanly in what he did to me in the hallway, but then I get distracted by the room I'm standing in.

Regardless of what he says about being a gentleman, the room is certainly fitted out like an English gentleman's club, with wood paneling, bookshelves full of books, armchairs, and a desk against one wall. The dark carpet is covered with silken rugs, and there's a drinks cabinet against one wall, a big oak wardrobe and drawers against the other. Another door is opposite.

"This doesn't look like a BDSM dungeon." I try to sound calm as I move over to the bookshelves and examine the books on them.

"It's not," Tate says. "It's my private office."

I turn to face him, my heart rate climbing as he closes the door.

No going back now.

"So," I say breathlessly. "Let's get this over with."

He examines me for a moment. "What exactly do you want to get over?"

"I said I didn't want to talk, Tate."

"But you should be here because you want to be, Katherine."

"I wouldn't be here if I didn't." The words come out sounding sharper than I intended, because I'm nervous. Just really fucking nervous.

Tate only stands there. "I need to hear you say it."

Oh, for God's sake. "Who knew there'd be so much talking involved?" I say, trying to be sarcastic, except the words come out thin and reedy-sounding. "Yes, I want to be here."

He tilts his head, studying me, and another helpless shiver chases over my skin. "Why?" he asks.

I'm losing patience, my nervousness increasing. "What do you mean, why? And what's with all the questions?"

"You should have said 'red' out in the hallway, but you didn't. Which means I can't do a scene with a sub who doesn't say their safe word when they should."

My mouth is dry. I don't like where this conversation is heading. It feels as if he's leading me into a trap, and I can sense the danger, I just don't know which direction it's coming from. "I didn't say it because I didn't want to," I say levelly. "It's not that deep."

He doesn't look away as he lifts a hand to the lock on the door and flicks it so it's closed. "You want to know what I do to subs who lie to me?" He takes a step toward me.

My heartbeat thuds loudly in my ears. "Why do you keep saying that? I'm not lying."

He ignores this, coming closer, stalking me like a panther. "I punish them, and usually in uncomfortable ways. Then again, perhaps you'll like the kinds of punishments I deal out."

"For the last time, I'm not lying."

"You're afraid, aren't you, sweet girl?" He stops not far

from where I'm standing near the bookshelves, his gaze relentless, and I find myself almost trembling yet again. "You're afraid of what you want."

I swallow. "Tate."

"You don't have to be afraid in here," he goes on, implacable. "I can give you what you want and what you need. I can give you everything."

"I don't—"

"Your safe word is 'red'. Say it for me now."

The breath goes out of me in a rush.

"Say it, Katherine."

His gaze is a pressure, a hand on the top of my head pushing me down, and my mouth opens before I can form a coherent thought. "'Red,'" I say.

Sparks glitter in his eyes. "Like I said out in the hallway, when you say that word, everything stops. It's for your safety and mine, but if you use it to manipulate me, I'll be very, *very* unhappy."

Okay, so this is happening.

All my nerves are tight. I'm keyed up and aware and really fucking tense. I don't know what the correct thing is to say, so I don't say anything at all.

Not that it matters, because Tate goes on, "You will address me as 'Sir'. You will not speak unless spoken to, and you will obey me as if you'd obey God himself. Is that clear?"

My heartbeat hammers away, my skin drawing tight and hot beneath my clothes. I'm aroused already, and my instinctive reaction is to fight it, to not let it get away on me, because who knows what will happen then?

I should speak, I should say something, but all I can manage is a hoarse "Okay."

His expression remains neutral. If he's satisfied by my

surrender, he gives no sign of it. "No," he corrects. "You say 'yes, Sir'.

This should feel like a cliche, a parody of itself, a farce even, yet it doesn't feel like any of those things. It feels dangerous, and he's radiating the kind of authority that makes my knees weak, and a part of me wants nothing more than to give him what he wants without a fight.

Yet I hate the thought of giving him all the control, of being helpless, and of being turned on by it the way I was in the hallway. That's not the part of me I want making decisions. That's the part I've been trying to distance myself from for ten years.

So why are you here then?

To face that part of me, perhaps. To overcome it.

"Yes, Sir," I say eventually.

His eyes narrow as if he's displeased with my tone, but he must have decided to let it go, because then he says, "Take your clothes off for me, sub. Do it slowly, then fold them neatly, and put them on the table near the door."

Get naked. Okay, so that's easy. I can do that, and it's not as if he hasn't seen my body before. Sure, it's been ten years, so I won't look the same as I did at nineteen, but too bad. He can deal.

I step out of my shoes, my pulse accelerating no matter what I tell myself about how ridiculous this is, then shrug out of my jacket. The shirt is next, and I undo the buttons, my fingers fumbling.

"Slowly, sub," Tate says. "I won't tell you again."

I grit my teeth at the order but try to slow down as I continue with the buttons. Only to have his hand suddenly cover both of mine. The shock of heat at his bare skin sends my heartbeat skyrocketing, and I freeze like a doe under the gaze of a lion.

"What do you say?" he asks softly.

I look up at him. "W-what do you mean?"

His gaze holds me trapped, the look in his eyes making goosebumps rise all over my skin. Fuck, he's so sexy I can't stand it. "When I give you an order, sub," he says, "You need to reply 'yes, Sir.'"

Okay, God. "Yes, Sir," I say.

Again, he gives me an assessing glance but then takes his hand away and nods. "Continue."

This time I remember to reply, "Yes, Sir."

He steps back, his arms folded over his chest, watching me.

It's difficult to undo the rest of my buttons with him looking at me like that, but I manage it. Then I take my shirt off, slip my skirt down, and carefully fold both of them. Standing in my underwear in front of Tate feels more exposing than I thought it would, my skin prickling and tightening as his gaze roves over me. But I don't let myself think about it too much as I take off my bra and step out of my underwear. Being naked is even more exposing. There's no way I can hide the hardening of my nipples, and he'll know exactly why they're hard, because it's not cold in the room.

Trying not to shake, I carry my stack of clothes over to the small console table by the door and put them down.

"Come here, sub," Tate orders.

"Yes, Sir," I say, moving over to where he's standing. I want to hold his gaze, show him that I'm not bothered by my nakedness or any of this, but I can't seem to make myself do it. The lines of his rough, handsome face are too hard, and his gaze is too intense, too fierce.

It reminds me of ten years ago, of how sometimes, when he looked at me, I had the sense that he wanted more than I was giving him, but I didn't understand what more he wanted. I didn't understand his anger at the world or why he was always so intense, and I still don't.

Perhaps it was this that he wanted. Me being submissive to him. Even now, I hate the thought, and I hate that I can't meet his gaze, either. It feels cowardly.

"Stand still," he orders. "I want to look at you."

"Yes, Sir." I stare at the floor, trying not to let the fact that he's studying every inch of my body affect me.

It's difficult, though, as he slowly paces a circle around me, looking at me from every angle. I feel like a goat tied to a stake, and he's a wolf, stalking me, deciding whether or not to eat me.

My skin gets even tighter, my breathing short and fast. I'm naked while he's fully clothed, and I feel vulnerable, so I have no idea why the pressure between my thighs tightens.

"You're a very pretty sub," Tate murmurs as he circles me yet again, then pauses directly behind me. "But I think you know that, don't you?"

"No," I say before I can stop myself. "I've never—"

A hand lands on my backside with a resounding crack, and I yelp in shock at the sting that follows in its wake. I start to turn, to shout at him for slapping me, but he's suddenly pressing against my spine, one hand at my throat, fingers circling my neck, his palm pressed to my pulse, the other hand on my stomach. His fingers are splayed, and he's holding me against him with irresistible strength.

I take another shocked breath at his grip and the furnace heat of his body against my back, at the prickle of wool from his suit jacket and pants against my tender skin. Already, I'm trembling at the possessiveness of his hold.

"That 'no' deserved a punishment," he murmurs in my ear, the prickle of his beard joining all the other prickling currently moving like static over my skin. "You're beautiful, sub. You've always been beautiful. And your skin is beautiful with the mark of my hand on it."

I'm breathing sharply, deep panting breaths, and I'm sure he can hear me. The sting on my backside has faded into a subtle heat that somehow feels good, but I can't work out why it would. I didn't realize that pain would be part of this.

"You didn't expect that, did you?" Tate breathes against my skin, again reading my mind. "But here's the thing, little sub. You ran away from me all those years ago, and no one runs away from me, not without a word or explanation."

I shut my eyes, a thread of panic winding through me. I don't want to talk about this, I don't want to go through it, not again. "I can't—"

"Did I ask you to speak?" he interrupts. "No, I did not. Only speak when spoken to, remember? Now, you're going to be punished, Katherine. You won't like the punishment, but you'll take it because I told you to."

His fingers flex around my throat, a subtle display of strength, of ownership, and hot, electric shivers crackle through my nerve endings. I don't want to like this, I don't want it to turn me on, yet it does.

"You can say your safe word at any time, remember?' he murmurs in my ear. "Do you want to say it now, sub?"

My brain is tripping and falling over itself, trying to make sense of what's happening. The slap on my ass. The mention of punishment. The reminder of the safe word. I could say it. I could. And all this confusion would end. I could walk out that door without looking back.

Then again, is this some kind of double bluff? I know he doesn't want me to leave, so is he expecting me to grit my way through it?

I don't want to do what he expects, yet I'm not sure there is any way to second-guess him. What I do know is that I'm certainly not going to give him the satisfaction of running like a coward.

"No, Sir," I say, making my voice sound cool and very level.

"Good," he says, and abruptly releases me, stepping away. "Stay there. Don't move a muscle."

I attempt to steady my frantic breathing, trying to pull myself together again. Behind me, I can hear Tate going over to the large cabinet standing against the wall and pulling out a drawer. I want to turn and see what he's doing, but he told me not to move, and so I stand there like an idiot, breathing too fast, my brain going round and around in circles.

Then I feel his heat behind me, and he's taking my wrists and pulling my arms behind me, and then comes the cool feel of leather against my skin and a feeling of pressure around my wrists.

Oh shit. Cuffs.

I catch my breath as the cuffs tighten, my wrists now securely fastened at the small of my back. I'm helpless. Completely and utterly helpless. The thread of panic winds tighter, but along with it comes that dark and dirty pleasure. My body likes the cuffs. It likes them very much.

Tate comes round to face me, his sharp green gaze cutting through me like a blade of pure emerald. "I told you that you wouldn't like it," he says. "But I think you like being cuffed, don't you?" Before I can reply, he takes a step, closing the distance between us, so he's right there, towering over me. And I feel his hand push between my thighs, his fingers stroking over my pussy, sending electric sparks everywhere. I gasp, tensing at the touch.

"I thought so." His voice is full of masculine satisfaction as he takes his hand away. "You're already wet and we haven't even started."

He lifts his hand to his mouth and licks my wetness from his fingertips with relish. "Nice," he murmurs approvingly. "You taste just as good as I remember."

My cheeks burn, but all he does is gesture to a spot on the floor in front of the armchair near his desk. "Kneel beside my armchair, sub. Eyes on the floor. Keep still."

"Yes, Sir," I parrot, hating how husky my voice is. But I don't want him to be right about me being scared, so I walk over to the spot he indicated, and then I kneel where he asked me to, staring at the floor.

He moves past me, over to the door, and unlocks it. Then, to my shock, he walks out without a backward glance, closing the door behind him.

9

Lucas

I finish up with Cherry by giving her a kiss for the pretty way she obeyed. She likes kissing, and I don't mind it with a sub who's been particularly good. But then she puts a hand on my chest and looks up at me. "You didn't come, Daddy," she says. "I'm sorry if I didn't give you what you needed."

Cherry is genuine in her submission. She wants the Doms to enjoy it as much as she does, and she knows I'm still hard. Unfortunately, that's not something I can hide from her since she's sitting in my lap.

"That's not on you," I say. "It's a problem with me. You were perfect."

She loves praise, and I can see that she's pleased with my answer. Yet there's still a little worry in her dark eyes. But I'm not talking about Katie with her — I don't talk about Katie with anyone — so instead I distract her with another kiss before sending her out of the playroom to get dressed.

I go over to the bed and pick up my jacket, my stupid fucking cock pressing hard against the zipper of my pants, making me furious at myself.

Katie was watching me, and knowing she was on the other side of that glass got me so fucking hard, so fucking quickly. I should have allowed myself to come with Cherry, because if I had, I wouldn't be so goddamn angry. But I didn't. I was fantasizing about her as I was fucking Cherry, and I knew if I kept going, I'd come quicker than I wanted to. It was distracting, and that wasn't fair to Cherry. Also, apart from anything else, I didn't want Katie to have that kind of power over me.

I never want *anyone* to have that kind of power over me, especially when I spent the first part of my life at the mercy of the foster system, bounced from one family to another. Last I counted, I'd been with fifteen different families before I got stuck in a group home. So, yeah, choice and control are important, which is probably why being a switch didn't work out for me.

I reach down and rearrange my stupid fucking dick, gritting my teeth as a flash of memory hits me. Of Cherry kneeling at my feet, with my cock in her mouth, and all I could think was, did Katie wish she was Cherry right now? Or was all of this turning her off completely?

I hope it didn't. I hope she fucking loved it.

The playroom door opens unexpectedly, and Tate walks in. "I need to talk to you," he says, closing the door after him.

"You better not need another fucking favor, because I'm all out of favors, right now."

"Pity," Tate says, his gaze level. "Because I was going to ask for one."

"No," I say curtly.

"You haven't heard what it is yet."

"I don't care."

He tilts his head. "You haven't asked me how Katherine found your demonstration."

"And I'm not going to." I'm terse, but that's all the emotional energy I have room for. "That's none of my fucking business."

"Actually, it is your business," Tate disagrees. "Because when I asked Katherine if she was thinking about you fucking her, she came so hard I thought the glass was going to break."

I go very still, looking at him. "She did?"

"Oh, yes," Tate says. "She got off on watching you. In fact, she was loving it. I only had to touch her clit once, and she went off like a fucking rocket."

This news does not make me feel any better, strangely enough, even if it is satisfying on some level. "Congratulations," I say. "Don't tell me, she changed her mind about a night."

Tate inclines his head. "She did. Thanks to you."

"You can send me roses later." I pick up my jacket from the bed. "Right now, I need a fucking drink."

"Luc," Tate says, his voice strangely intense. "The favor I need to ask, I think you'll like."

I throw my jacket over my shoulder. "I'm not fucking another sub for you."

"Not even if the sub is Katherine?" Tate asks.

It takes a lot to surprise me. A lot more to shock me, but I'm shocked right now. It's as if I've taken hold of a live wire. "What?" I ask, because surely I've misheard.

"It worked well out in the hallway." Tate meets my gaze head-on. "She loved watching you, and she wants a night. But she's afraid, and I don't know what of, so I need to be careful. I don't want to push too hard and end up frightening her away."

I stare back. "What do you want?" I snap. "Be fucking clear, Tate."

"I want you and me to work together," he says. "In a scene with her."

For the first time in my messy goddamn life, I'm speechless. All I can do is stare as my brain tries to process what he's just said.

"I know you want her," Tate goes on. "And she wants you, too. "

"Jesus." I run a distracted hand through my hair. "Did she tell you that?"

"No. But her pussy doesn't lie."

Something inside me shifts and turns, growling. Something hungry. "Are you serious?" I demand, my temper pulling at the leash. "And don't fucking lie to me, Tate."

"I'm not." He just looks at me steadily. "I want to make this scene the best it can be, and for that, I need you."

I get turned on by subs all the time, a hard-on isn't anything new, and I've had vanilla sex with a lot of different women. Pick-ups in bars, work colleagues, and the occasional friend with benefits. All sex without strings or commitments.

But I've never done a scene with a woman I actually feel something for, still less what I feel for Katie, and it's dangerous. This whole thing feels dangerous. Yet, I know I'm not going to refuse. I *know*. Because Tate is right, he can push too hard sometimes, and given how he feels about her, the possibility he might frighten her away is a valid concern. My presence tempers him, helps him find a middle ground, and subs find me reassuring.

Fuck, I can't say no, not when it's her. Not when her pleasure and well-being are the most important things here. It's not about me. It *can't* be about me.

"You really want me in on this?' I ask. "Because once I'm in, that's it. You can't change your mind. It'll be between us forever."

He doesn't flinch. "Yes, I know. But if I want to keep her this time, I'm going to have to find out what she's hiding, because she *is* hiding something. Something that was between us in our marriage ten years ago, and I need to know what it is. I need you to help me unlock her."

"Perhaps what was between you and her in your marriage was me," I challenge, because if he's asking this of me and if we're talking about it now, we're going to fucking talk.

"Maybe," Tate says without heat. "But I think it's about more than just that."

Fuck. He doesn't seem at all bothered about the thought of Katie and me. Still, there's a truth he needs to know, and I have to be straight with him. "If I help you, Tate, then it won't just be 'my' problem anymore. It'll be yours too. Because if I have her, I'm not going to want to let her go, either."

This time, his gaze flickers. But only for a second. "I hear you. We'll sort that out later. She's waiting for us now."

Anticipation is gathering in my gut, my cock by now painfully hard. The thought of having her, after so long... Fuck, I'm not going to refuse, no matter how difficult it makes things between Tate and me. I can't.

"You tell her that I'm coming?"

"No," he says. "I want it to be a surprise, to unsettle her."

"Is that the best idea right now?"

"Perhaps not," he admits. "But the only way she'll allow herself to have any kind of pleasure is if I order her to. And I think she'll resist. Fuck, she's resisting now."

There are questions I want to ask him, things to get straight before I involve myself, but we could talk about this all night, and I can tell he's already impatient to be back in that room with her.

And so are you.

Yeah, I am. And I'm done talking about it.

"Okay," I say, dumping the jacket so I can roll down my sleeves and do up my cuffs, desire winding tighter and tighter through me. "Let's do this."

10

Katherine

Tate's been gone a while. Longer than I thought he'd be. I'm starting to look around the room, wondering if he'd really notice if I moved, and where the fuck did he go anyway, when the door opens again.

"Eyes on the floor, sub," Tate orders as he comes back in.

"Yes, Sir." I look at the carpet in front of me.

Then I hear another footstep. The quality of the air in the room changes, thickening, becoming dense and electric, like a storm about to break.

He's got someone else in here, hasn't he? There's someone else in the room, and they're looking at me. They're looking at me while I'm naked and handcuffed.

I jerk my head up, unable to help myself, and all the breath leaves my lungs.

It's Lucas. It's fucking Lucas and he's in here too, and his golden gaze meets mine, and instantly it feels as if all the tension in the room is concentrated in the air between us. A crackling energy that makes my whole body tense.

"Eyes on the fucking ground, sub," Tate growls in warning.

I tear my gaze from Lucas's, staring at the floor instead, my heartbeat racing out of control. Why is Lucas here? Tate must have asked him to be, but why? Does Tate know about my feelings for him?

Imagine yourself coming around Lucas's cock...

Tate's voice whispers in my head, and suddenly I can't breathe, my face hot, the throb between my thighs intensifying. I can imagine it. I can imagine it all too clearly. Oh God, this is going to be too much for me, I just know it.

"Master Lucas will be joining us," Tate says, his voice closer as he comes over to the armchair that I'm kneeling in front of. "You will obey him as you obey me." He's standing in front of me. I can see the polished black leather of his shoes. "You want to safe word, sub?"

I could. I could say 'red' now, and it would stop. I could leave and go back to my apartment and my job, and pretend Tate didn't make me come in the hallway and that Lucas didn't see me naked and kneeling on the floor, my hands cuffed behind my back.

But my mouth won't form the word. Saying it would be giving in, would be letting both of them know I can't handle this, that I'm just as much of a coward now as I was back then, letting that one awful experience ruin sex for me forever, and I can't do it. So, no. I'm not going to say it.

"No, Sir," I manage to get out.

"Good." Lucas's voice is warm, but I can hear the authority in it. There's a gentler edge to his than Tate's, and my breath catches hard. He's coming closer too, I can feel it, and then he's standing beside me. He's just out of my field of vision, but I'm so hyper aware of him that I can sense him. I can feel him staring too, a pressure at the back of my head. "You may address me as Daddy," he says, and my face gets even hotter. Daddy? Fucking Daddy? It sounds wrong, ridiculous even, yet there's nothing ridiculous about the nervous anticipation gathering inside me. About how I can feel the two of them staring down at me.

Two men? What a little whore.

Just as the insidious voice of my mother whispers in my head, warm fingers grip the back of my neck in a strong, possessive hold. It's him. It's Lucas. "What do you say, sub?" he asks softly. "Master Tate must have taught you some manners. Don't disappoint him."

I swallow, my mouth as dry as the desert. "Y-yes, D-daddy," I force out, part of me cringing at the word, even as other parts of me want to press myself into his grip.

"Nice." The warmth is back in his voice again. "A good sub." He lets go of the back of my neck and runs his fingertips down my spine in a feather-light touch, and my whole body trembles in reaction.

I always treated him as my closest friend, even when I knew that what I felt for him wasn't friendship, but there's nothing friendly in that touch. It's deliberate, intentional, and my response to it is helpless. I can't hide it from him, and I can't hide it from Tate, and I don't know how I'm going to get through this now. I'm used to hiding, to running away when things get uncomfortable, and this is very, *very* uncomfortable.

But I already decided I wouldn't say my safe word when Lucas walked in, and I'm not going to say it now just because he touched me. If Tate is hoping to push me by adding Lucas to the mix, I won't give him the satisfaction.

"A drink?" Tate asks above my head.

"Sure," Lucas answers, and I watch his shoes move away to the armchair opposite Tate's. He sits down, his long legs stretched out in front of him, and I hear Tate go over to the drinks cabinet.

"Sub," he says as he gets out a bottle and two tumblers. "Go and show Master Lucas how pretty you are."

Instantly, my breathing gets short and sharp. Show him? What does he mean by 'show him'? How do I do that?

"Don't think," Tate says, seeing my hesitation. "Just do it."

"Yes, Sir," I say hoarsely, and force myself to my feet.

I don't want to see the expression on Lucas's face. I don't want to know what he thinks about this at all, so I don't look at him as I move over to where he's sitting, keeping my attention on the carpet. I'm unsure about what to do next, but Lucas isn't. He sits up, spreading his knees, reaching for my hips. "Let's have a look at you," he murmurs, the shock of his hands on my bare skin making my breath catch as he pulls me closer, so I'm standing between his thighs. He's looking at me, I can feel the pressure of his gaze, but I still can't look back. He was a friend, but he's very much not now, and my face feels like it's on fire, a pulsing throb between my thighs.

I always wanted him to look at me, and now he is, but Tate is right there, and I have no idea what to do with myself.

"Very pretty. Very pretty indeed," he says, and it should be patronizing as hell, yet a stupid part of me glows like the sun at the approval in his voice.

"Look at me, sub," he orders.

I don't want to. I don't want to look at him, have the electricity that has always been between us become real, yet there's no escaping it if I don't want to use my safe word. If I want to prove to both of them, and to myself, that I can handle this.

So slowly, I lift my gaze to his, only to find myself caught there, a fly in a spider's web, unable to get away.

His eyes are bright gold and they're blazing, fierce with anger and desire, and other things too complicated for me to work out. But God, he's beautiful. He makes my heart beat just as fast Tate does.

"You're forgetting something," he says, chiding.

Oh fuck. "Yes, Daddy," I say, and I don't even cringe a little as I say it.

"Good girl." His gaze slowly drops down my body as he studies me. My nipples have gone hard, and it's impossible to hide them, just as it's impossible to hide how fast I'm breathing. "Turn around. Show me those wrists."

"Yes, Daddy." I swallow and turn my back to him, my brain running in frantic circles again. Is he going to make me suck him off like he did with Cherry? With Tate in the room? I feel hot all over at the thought.

"Nice," he murmurs, and I feel him tug gently on the

short chain connecting each cuff, then drop a hand to the curve of my bare ass, stroking lightly. I can't stop the hiss of breath in my throat as he touches me. It's so loud in the room I want to cringe. "Responsive, too. Turn around, please."

"Yes, Daddy." This time, I try to get myself together as I turn back to him, to not be so rabbit-in-the-headlights. But it's impossible, because he lifts a hand and brushes the backs of his fingers over the curls between my thighs. The touch is light, gentle, yet it makes me shiver like a tree in a high wind. "Natural redhead," he says. "I always wondered."

Tate comes over and puts a tumbler of amber liquid on the little table beside Lucas's armchair. "Beautiful, yes?" he says casually.

"Very," Lucas replies. "Slippery pussy too, from what I can see."

My face burns at the frankness of their conversation. Lucas can see how turned on I am just standing in front of him while he examines me, and I'm embarrassed about it. I'm embarrassed to be feeling anything at all if I'm honest.

He strokes the backs of his fingers over the curls between my thighs yet again, and again, I tremble help-lessly. "Is that for me, sub?' he asks, his golden eyes looking up into mine. "Is that all for me?"

No, I want to say. No, it's not for you, it's just my stupid body being a little slut. But that's not what comes out of my mouth. "Yes, Daddy," I whisper instead.

"You might want to see to that," Tate says absently, turning away and going back to his armchair before sitting down.

Lucas turns me around, then pulls me back with a gentle, irresistible force until I'm sitting in his lap. It's awkward with my hands behind my back, and I stiffen, my

94

breathing hoarse. Except then his fingers push into my hair, closing into a fist, and he's tugging my head back until I'm resting back against him, my head on his shoulder. Then he holds me there as his free hands slides beneath one of my thighs, lifting it and draping it over the arm of his chair, before doing the same thing with the other thigh.

I stiffen further in instinctive anxiety, painfully aware of how I must look lying against Lucas with my legs spread wide and held open by the arms of the chair. Vulnerable. Exposed. And Tate, sitting opposite, watching us, his expression inscrutable.

This feels so wrong, dirty, and confusing to be positioned like this. And I can't move. I can't close my legs or use my hands to push myself away. His fingers gripping my hair keep exactly where I am, and I'm so turned on I can barely speak.

"You're very tense, sub," Lucas says. "Is there something you want to say?"

My safe word, presumably. Except I'm not going to say it. I'm not going to acknowledge any of those confusing, awful feelings, not in any way.

"No, Daddy," I say, trying to keep my voice steady.

Tate's gaze shifts from me to Lucas, and some kind of wordless communication passes between them that makes me tense even more.

Yet Lucas only says, "I want you to lie still, just like this, and to stay quiet. Don't make a sound. Can you do that, sub?"

"Y-yes, Daddy," I stutter.

He takes a sip of his drink, then he and Tate start talking idly about the club, about overheads and tax breaks, and donations. But as they talk, Lucas's fingers casually stroke over my stomach, making me shudder, then push through the curls between my thighs to the wet, sensitive flesh of my pussy.

The breath hisses between my gritted teeth as he touches me, a jolt of hot pleasure making a gasp catch in my throat. His fingertips brush my clit, oh so lightly, and the jolt becomes an electric shock. Then his other hand strokes down the side of one breast before cupping it and squeezing it gently. His thumb strokes over my painfully hard nipple, pinching lightly, and I almost gasp aloud. He does it again and again, and the shocks of pleasure become more and more intense.

I set my jaw, trying to stop the whimper that pushes against my teeth, threatening to escape. I'm achingly aware of the arms of the chair pressing against the backs of my thighs and his fingers in my hair. My hands are behind me in the cuffs, and the feeling of being restrained makes everything more acute.

Why do I like being held down like this? Why is Tate watching Lucas toy with me such a turn-on? Why does the fact that Lucas is touching me make me want more and more and more?

'Dirty little slut,' my mother shouts at me. 'What do you think you were doing? Flaunting yourself, weren't you?'

I wasn't flaunting myself. I was just talking. That asshole was the one who pushed me up against the wall, and he was the one who kissed me. I didn't ask him to. I didn't want it. I didn't.

But I want this. I can't fight the relentless build of pleasure as his fingers stroke me, exploring between my thighs with a delicacy that makes me want to moan. I lose track of their conversation, too busy trying not to make a sound as he continues to play, one long finger sliding around and over my clit, and I shift under his touch, unable to help myself.

His body is so hot beneath me, and I can feel how hard he is. Yet he's talking to Tate, lounging in the armchair opposite, as if the pair of them are having a fucking office meeting.

I shake and shake as Lucas's finger finds the slick entrance to my body and eases in, his thumb pressing on my clit, but adding only pressure. No friction except for the lazy slide of his finger in and out of me.

I forget about fighting, my hips lifting to his hand, a whimper escaping me.

"Ssh," he growls softly in my ear. "What did I say?"

His breath is warm on my skin, and he smells good. Cedar maybe, or sandalwood, but it's not like Tate's. His scent is warm and delicious, and I don't want to like it, but I do. His body is as hard as Tate's, but leaner, and the press of his cock is insistent. Yet there's no impatience to him. It's as if he could fondle me all day, without any urgency.

"Answer me," he orders, low and soft, his authority irresistible.

"You s-said to be quiet and k-keep still," I force out.

"I did," he agrees. "And are you doing what I said?"

"Is she being disobedient?" Tate asks.

"I have it in hand," Lucas replies, and he's being quite literal as his finger pushes into me yet again.

I shudder, another moan trying to break free. "N-no, I'm not."

"No," he agrees. "You're not. So, keep quiet until I say, hmm?"

I shut my eyes, trying to concentrate on keeping quiet. "Y-yes, Daddy."

"That's a good girl." His voice is a purr in my ear. "And I

don't want you coming before I say. That will earn my displeasure, and you don't want that." Then, to emphasize his point, he adds another finger.

I try to swallow another moan as he fucks me with his fingers, knowing I can't pull away. I can't do anything but lie against him and take it, and it's so good, a raw, aching pleasure, that makes my thinking processes fracture under the weight of it.

They're still talking, but I don't hear them. Every little movement of Lucas's fingers is driving me insane. I so desperately want to come, except he told me not to, and all I can think about is how I want to please him. How I want to be his good girl. So I bite my lip bloody trying to hold back the orgasm, my body trembling uncontrollably.

"I don't think she's going to make it," Tate observes from his armchair. "Little sub is too greedy."

"Oh, I think she will," Lucas says, pushing down on my clit with his thumb, even as his long fingers slide into my pussy. "You don't want to be a bad girl for Daddy, do you, sub?"

I'm panting, I can't help it. "N-no, no," I babble. "No, Daddy."

Tate pushes himself out of his armchair, strolling over to where Lucas and I are sitting. He stops before the chair and folds his arms across his broad chest, green eyes clinical as he looks down at me. But I can see his cock pushing against the zipper of his pants. He's not as immune as he looks, and for some reason, knowing that makes me relax a little. I don't want to be the only one affected by this.

"She is a bad girl, though," Tate says in a hard voice. "She ran away from me. She ran away from *us*. And I don't think we can let that slide, can we, Luc?"

"No," Lucas says, nuzzling against my ear. "I don't think

we can." He takes his fingers from between my thighs and then lifts them to my lips, pushing them into my mouth, making me taste myself along with the salt of his skin.

I give another helpless whimper.

"It's a shame we have to punish you, because I love a soaking wet pussy," he says. "But as Tate says, you need to be taught a lesson, little girl." He takes his hand away and releases my hair, and as he does so, Tate reaches for me, pulling me upright in Lucas's lap. Lucas's hands are moving beneath me, a belt buckle being undone, a zipper coming down. Oh God. I know what's going to happen next. He's going to fuck me in front of Tate.

Nervous anticipation winds tighter inside me, along with a wild heat that makes me panic. Not about the awful feelings, though. I'm panicking because I'm not going to be able to hold back the orgasm. The moment he slides inside me, I'm going to come, and then I'll be punished. I have no idea what the punishment will be, but it might be like that slap Tate gave me before, and I don't want that.

I'm already panting and trembling by the time I hear the crinkle of a foil packet, the shivers getting worse.

"You already got an orgasm out there in the hallway," Tate says. "Fantasizing about coming all over his cock. So now it's his turn. If you come before him, you're going to have to deal with me."

I want to say no, to say stop, because I'm not going to be able to hold back the climax I can sense just out of reach. "I...c-can't," I stutter hoarsely. "I'm not going to—"

"Be quiet," Tate orders. "You can say your safe word, but that's the only thing I want to hear from you." He leans down, his hard, green eyes inches from mine. "Unless you want to tell me just what the hell you're so afraid of."

Except I can't think with him looking at me like that, and

JACKIE ASHENDEN

I certainly don't want to tell him anything, so I stare back, giving a slight shake of my head.

"Stubborn, girl," Tate murmurs. "Show her what bratty subs get, Luc."

Lucas grips my hips, holding me in place as he leans forward. "I want you to keep, very, very still, little sub," he purrs, his voice soft and warm as liquid honey. "Because I've been thinking about this pussy for the past ten years, and it's my turn. So, I don't want you sneaking in another orgasm before I'm ready to give you one, hmm?"

I'm quivering with anticipation, my breath stuck in my throat. I can't speak, yet from somewhere I dredge up the words he wants to hear. "Y-yes Daddy."

Then, before I can say anything else, I feel the push of his cock against my slippery, throbbing flesh. A cry is torn from my throat as my pussy stretches around him. He's sliding deep inside me, and he's big, and I had so many fantasies about him doing just this, and it feels so good I can't stand it. The way he was touching me just before had me already on the edge of coming as it was, and no amount of fighting is going to stop the orgasm that rolls over me now, relentless as a freight train.

"Bad girl," Lucas says roughly, his fingers gripping tight to my hips as I pulse helplessly around him, shuddering and shaking. "I expressly told you not to come."

But there's nothing I can do but cry out as pleasure explodes through my entire body. And then Tate grips my jaw, leaving me with no choice but to look at him, and before I can fully process what's happening, he leans forward and covers my mouth with his.

It's a raw, hungry kiss, just like the kisses he used to give years ago. Hot, insistent, demanding. His tongue is in my mouth, exploring, and I can taste the clean, alcoholic flavor of the vodka he's been drinking, and my head spins.

I'm full of disappointment at myself for not being able to hold back, for not being able to resist the pleasure, and disobeying them. Now, I'll be punished.

Tate lifts his head just as I'm leaning helplessly into him, wanting more of that kiss. "Disobedient sub," he says, his stare fierce. "Showing me up like in front of Master Lucas. Well, I told you that if you disobeyed, you'd have to deal with me."

Lucas hasn't moved, his long, thick cock still deep inside me, but his hands move from my hips and up my sides, sliding around to cup my breasts, pinching my hard nipples.

I jerk as pleasure/pain sparks through my body, even as I stammer, "I t-tried, Sir. But I—"

"I don't want to hear excuses." Tate's hands drop to his belt, and he starts undoing it. "You got greedy." He pulls down his zipper. "So now you're going to pay for it."

Oh God. I'm breathing faster again, my pulse ramping up as he reaches down and pulls his cock out. It's just as hard and thick and long as I remember, and I can't hear anything through the hammering of my heartbeat.

"I want you to suck me off until I come," Tate orders. 'But again, if you come again before I do, then there will be consequences."

As if in warning, Lucas's hands on my breasts squeeze gently, his hips beginning to move, and I gasp as another jolt of pleasure hits me. "Y-yes, Sir," I manage to force out, my attention focused on the way Tate is gripping his cock in one large fist.

"You've been warned." He steps closer, slides one hand into my hair, pulling me forward. "Open up," he says, then guides his cock into my mouth with the other.

He's hot against my tongue, all smooth skin and salt, and the taste of him is all Tate. Familiar. He really liked me giving him blow jobs on my knees, and again, all those old, conflicting feelings of being turned on and yet dirty at the same time threaten to return.

It's worse this time, though, because I'm not in control of this. I'm not in control of any of this, and a dim part of me is panicking. Especially when Lucas's hands move me the way he wants as he thrusts into me, the slide of his cock already driving me towards another peak, and then Tate's dick filling my mouth, his grip on my hair tightening, holding me still.

It's overwhelming being caught between them and having them both inside me at the same time, and it's so wrong that I'm completely at their mercy, yet it feels so good. Too good.

I want to close my eyes so Tate can't see the conflict waging a war inside me, but naturally, he spots my urge to hide. "Don't you dare," he murmurs roughly. "Eyes on me when you're sucking my cock, sub."

I can't say anything, not with my mouth full of him. All I can do is try to overcome my gag reflex as he thrusts deeper into my mouth, brushing the back of my throat.

My world narrows to the thrust of Tate's cock in my mouth, the slide of Lucas's dick in my pussy, and the heat in Tate's eyes. It's so good. It's so intense, and there's nothing I can do to make it easier, to reduce it somehow, make it manageable. And I'm nearly coming again, which makes me tear up. Because I'm not going to be able to stop it this time either, just like I couldn't with the last, and all my fighting, all my resistance is for nothing.

Then just as I'm about to burst into sobs, Tate's gaze flickers and he growls, "Come for him, sub. Come all over his cock. *Now*."

As soon as the words are out of his mouth, my body relaxes and I let the second orgasm crush me, a muffled scream vibrating against Tate's cock in my mouth. Lucas thrusts harder, timing his with Tate's, but I'm already flying. Dimly, I hear Lucas curse, and his body shudders. Then Tate slides both hands into my hair, gripping me tightly as he fucks my mouth until he's growling as he empties himself down the back of my throat.

11

Tate

Lucas deals with the condom, then tugs Katherine back against his chest. She's got her eyes closed, her hair half coming out of her little bun, tears and mascara running down her face, and she's never looked so lovely to me. Having her mouth around my dick, sucking me the way she used to, but this time not pulling away when things got too intense, just staring up at me as she swallowed me, was as good as I thought it would be. No, it's fucking better.

She surrendered to Lucas and me so beautifully, and watching him toy with her, watching her shift and bite her lip and whimper as he stroked her pretty little cunt, was fucking hot.

It was a calculated risk asking Lucas to join us, but I knew that after the way she came against my fingers while watching him with Cherry, that maybe he had to be part of this too. He's always tempered my impatience, provided reassurance when I don't want to give it, and stops me from pushing too hard, too soon. We work well together as Doms, and part of me has been wondering if the missing link between Katherine and me, all those years ago, was Lucas.

Anyway, given her resistance to me and her determination not to acknowledge her own arousal, to pretend that giving me her submission was something casual, I knew I had to do something. I didn't want to scare her, that's the last thing I wanted to do. I wanted to give her pleasure, show her that her sexuality and the intensity of what we shared all those years ago were nothing to be ashamed of. I wanted to fix what was wrong between us.

So, asking Lucas for his help seemed like the most logical thing to do. Also, he wants her. Of course, again, it was risky to ask him, because he's as possessive as I am, and he made it very clear that if he joined the scene, he wasn't likely to let her go afterward either.

That's an issue, but since Katherine and her needs were more important in the immediate present than anything else, I decided I'd deal with that later.

Initially, when Lucas came in and I saw her shock at his presence, I wondered if I'd miscalculated, and she was going to say her safe word. But she didn't. And when he ordered her to come to him, she went, and seeing him with his hand between her thighs, and how wet she was, I knew that having him join us was the right thing to do.

I tuck myself away, then go to the small ensuite bathroom I had put in when the club was being built and run some warm water over a small cloth. Then I go back into the office and over to Lucas's chair, taking Katherine's stubborn, pointed chin in gentle fingers and cleaning up her face.

Lucas is busy taking the pins out of her hair and combing his fingers through her long, red curls, letting them cascade over his shoulder and the arm of the chair. She doesn't move as I wipe the tears from her cheeks, lying lax with her eyes closed against Lucas's chest.

He gives me a direct look, but he doesn't have to speak in order to tell me what he's thinking right now. I know already. Fucking her has only cemented his need for her, as I knew it would. He's not going to give her up to me without a fight.

Naturally, I have no intention of giving her to him, either, but that's something we'll discuss later, in private. I stare back, and he gives a slight nod, getting the picture. Then he glances down at Katherine. "Wrists," he says.

I move to shift her slightly, so I can check on the cuffs and make sure her blood flow is good, and it is. There's no reason to take them off just yet, and I like having her cuffed. She likes it too, no matter how she denies it.

"All good," I say. "Let's leave them on."

Lucas nods again, then pushes a curl back from Katherine's forehead. "Wake up now, pretty sub," he murmurs. "Tate has some questions he needs answered, and then there's the other question of punishments."

She stirs against him, reluctant to open her eyes. So, I order, "Open your eyes, sub. Now."

This time she opens them immediately, looking first up

at Lucas and then at me. Her blue gaze is dark and deep, and wide, and for a second, I see pain there. Then the shutters come down, wariness entering her eyes. She shifts in Lucas's arms, but instantly, he closes his fingers in her hair into a fist, keeping her where she is. "No," he murmurs. "Stay still, little girl."

A breath escapes her, and she trembles, but doesn't fight. Her breasts are rising and falling fast, though, her soft pink nipples in hard little points. She really loves being restrained, and it's obvious.

"What is this?" she asks. "Good Dom, bad Dom?"

I smile at this display of spirit, because I like her fight. I always did, even if it scared her. "Talking back already, sub? If you're not careful, that might just earn you another punishment."

Her mouth firms, as if she wants to protest, but all she says is, "Sorry, Sir."

"I don't think you are, but let's leave that for the moment." I put the cloth down on the floor. "I want to know why you left, Katherine. And I want the truth."

She shifts on Lucas again, hissing at the grip Lucas has on her hair, but he doesn't let up. It's good. She needs to know there's no escape. That she's held and contained here by us. She could safe out, of course, and then I'd lose her, but given the pleasure she's already had at our hands, and how much she loved that, I'm gambling that she won't.

"Does it matter?" There's an edge in her voice. "It was ten years ago."

"It matters." I hold her gaze. "I loved you, Katherine. And you left without a word or an explanation."

Her lashes fall at this, and her cheeks flush. "I'm sorry. I just didn't love you the way you—"

"No," I interrupt. "That's not the reason. And I told you not to lie to me."

Flickers of her fiery temper glitter in her eyes. "Are we doing this Dom thing or what? Because that's what I signed on for, not fucking conversation."

Lucas's fingers tighten further, pulling at her hair, making her gasp. "Language, little sub," he murmurs. "You need to show some respect for Master Tate."

"You do," I agree. "You're already up for some punishments. I'm sure you don't want any more."

She bites her lip, her body quivering. "Yes, Sir," she whispers.

It's clear that she's not going to give in, not yet, so I glance at Lucas to give him the green light to move her for the next part of the scene. He lets her go, and now it's my turn to take her in my arms.

She's warm and soft against my chest, the scent of flowers and sweet feminine musk sending me back ten years to when I first held her. When I first kissed her, and felt something in me, something that had been sleeping all this time, wake up.

That same thing is still there, still awake, and still waiting for her, and I feel the clench of it now as her lashes lift and she looks up at me. Her gaze is full of trepidation and wariness, and yet beneath all of that, I see her hunger. It's the reason she hasn't said her safe word yet, and I know that. There's always been a hunger in her, desperate and wild, and she's afraid of it. She's afraid of giving in to it. But she has to understand that she can give that hunger to me. I will sate it. I will show her that it's okay to surrender to it. That it's not wrong to feel the things she feels, because I'm starting to wonder if that was her problem all along. If that's why she left.

"It's okay to give in to it, sub," I say as I move over to my armchair. "It's okay to lose yourself. I'm here to catch you, and so is Lucas."

The color in her face deepens, and she looks away, hiding from me again. She won't for too much longer, though. I'll make sure of it. I'll make sure she gives me everything.

I sit down in the armchair, with her in my lap. The arms of the chair are low and padded to my specifications, and perfect for doling out punishments on a sub's backside. I arrange her, turning her onto her stomach so her pretty ass is exposed. Lucas comes to the side of the chair and kneels to grip her legs, so she doesn't kick. She tenses up, but I'm not making any allowances tonight. Besides, the feeling of being restrained should make this intense and pleasurable for her, though she won't enjoy it at first.

"I have to punish you, sub," I tell her. "Firstly, because you ran away from us, and secondly because you didn't give us an explanation. And also, because you made us wait ten fucking years before coming back, and that's just not acceptable. So now you're going to get the spanking you so richly deserve."

I don't wait.

I bring the flat of my hand down on her ass.

12

Katherine

I'm face down across Tate's hard thighs, one of his hands on the back of my neck, holding me down as he brings the other down hard on my butt. He's not light or gentle, and there's strength behind it. He really means it. This is a punishment.

And it hurts. It fucking hurts.

More tears start in my eyes, and I gasp at the pain and the stinging heat prickling over my skin. I want to flinch or kick, but Lucas is holding my legs in an iron grip, and again, I can't move. It makes that dark, dirty hunger coil so tight right down low inside me.

"What do you say?" Tate demands. "Thank me for it, sub."

"T-thank you, Sir," I say hoarsely. It should worry me how automatic it is to do what he says, but I'm too busy steeling myself for the next blow to worry. Too busy processing the pain.

He brings his palm down again, and again I gasp, yet more tears making my vision waver. "Say thank you," he demands again, and again, I do.

You shouldn't have left the way you did.

I know. Deep in my heart, I know. But it was for him as much as it was for me. I thought it would make him happier if I were gone. I thought it would be better for his friendship with Lucas, too.

I grit my teeth as he brings his palm down on my ass, one cheek and then another, and I thank him in a shaky voice each time. He pauses between strikes to slide his fingers between my thighs, pinching and pressing on my clit, adding raw pleasure to the relentless pain, until I'm no longer sure which is which.

Oh God, I can't believe I'm getting off on this, but I am. Just another example of how warped my sexuality truly is.

I can't stop from shifting on his thighs, my back arching as I try to avoid the blows, but I can't. Just as I can't avoid the stroke of his fingers, pleasure and pain twining tighter and tighter around each other.

'You're not going to do that again, are you, sub?" Tate

demands as he delivers another blow. "You're not going to run off without an explanation."

"No," I force out, my voice hoarse. "No, Sir."

"You're going to tell us what's bothering you, what's hurting you, and what you're afraid of, aren't you, sub?"

I shut my eyes, tears leaking from beneath my lids, and not only because of physical pain, but because there's a tense knot of emotions sitting in my chest too. A truth I can't run from, not anymore.

I hurt him when I left. He loved me, and I took his choice away from him, just as Mom's hookup took my choice from me. I left him with no explanation and no further contact, and I can make all the excuses in the world that it was for him, but really, it was for myself.

Because I was a coward.

"Yes, S-Sir." I start to sob as a strange rush of emotion overwhelms me, tears dripping onto the carpet. "I'm sorry, Sir. I didn't mean to. I'm so sorry."

The blows stop all of a sudden, Lucas's grip on my legs loosening. Then Tate turns me over on his lap and puts his arms around me, holding me the way Lucas held me, tight against his chest. My ass is burning, and the pressure between my thighs is still intense, and the pressure in my chest, from all the emotions I buried there a long time ago, is making it so I can't breathe.

"Good," he says approvingly, stroking my hair. "Obedient, sub. You took your punishment well and a very pretty apology, too. We're going to get to the bottom of this, though. You're going to tell us your secrets eventually, but for now, you can have a reward. Do you agree, Master Lucas?"

"I do," Lucas says, rising to his feet. "And I know just what kind of reward she'll enjoy."

Tate shifts me again in his lap, his knees spreading my thighs wide apart and holding them there. I tremble as Lucas kneels in front of the armchair, between my legs, because I know what's going to happen next and part of me is desperate for it, while the other part, the part I've never managed to leave behind me, is instinctively ashamed of my own neediness.

Lucas's amber gaze holds mine as he grips my thighs tightly. "You're going to come, sub, and come hard no matter how hard you fight." It's both a threat and a warning, and I'm only just processing it when he leans in and his mouth covers my pussy, and I arch helplessly against Tate, a hoarse cry escaping me.

Tate grips the cuffs at my back, restraining me still further, and Lucas's hands increase the sense of restriction. I'm trembling as his tongue pushes into me, going slow, taking his time as he tastes me, and I jerk in Tate's grip. I can't hide how much this is getting me off, and I can't bite back the moans that press against my teeth.

"Let Master Lucas know how much you're enjoying this, sub." Tate's deep voice is at my ear, his mouth brushing over my neck the way he did out in the hallway. "You watched him eat Cherry out and now he's going to do the same to you, and you love it, don't you?"

I'm barely listening, because Lucas's tongue is relentless, circling my clit, his teeth against my labia, making me shake and shake, that dark pleasure coiling tight and hot inside me.

"Answer me," Tate insists.

"Yes, Sir," I pant just as Lucas's tongue pushes into me again, and the pant turns into a cry and a gasp as he goes deeper.

"Nice," Tate says. "Again." And this time, his large hand

cups one breast, and he pinches my nipple, delivering more pain with my pleasure.

I give a hoarse scream, and he does it again, and again, timing it with the flicks of Lucas's tongue, until I'm a writhing, gasping mess in his arms. I don't think it's possible to come again, and yet here I am, on the verge of yet another orgasm, and so quickly. So easily. It was always easy with Tate, and now adding Lucas to the mix has made it even easier.

"Don't be afraid of what you feel, little sub," Tate murmurs, the prickle of his beard against the side of my neck. "This is what we like, what gets us off. Watching you come, getting overwhelmed by pleasure. This is why we do what we do. It's for you. It's all for you."

His words slowly penetrate the haze of pleasure, and even though I barely take them, they settle down inside me. This gives them pleasure. *My* pleasure gives them pleasure. They don't judge me. They *want* me to feel it, so why am I fighting it?

Lucas and I will catch you...

That's what Tate said, and I didn't understand it a few moments ago, but now I do. I can give myself up to them and not worry about being overwhelmed by it or afraid of losing control to it. Because they're there to hold me, to keep me contained. To keep me safe.

And just like that, it's easy to let go. Easy to stop fighting, to give myself up to the pleasure that Lucas's wicked tongue is giving me, and the sharp, bright pain that Tate's hands on my breasts are doling out. Not a bad pain, a good pain. And I admit to myself that I like that I can't move. I like that I can do nothing but take what they give, because I'm not responsible for it. They are.

They hold the reins, and all I want is to go where they lead me.

"Come for us, sub," Tate growls in my ear. "Come for us, now."

I do, because Lucas's tongue gives me one last flick over my clit and I'm flying, pleasure exploding through me like a lightbulb popping and shattering, electricity lighting me up.

The room echoes with the sounds of my screams, and then I'm slumping back against Tate's chest, his powerful arms around me. I keep my eyes closed, not wanting to move — not that I could even if I wanted to — hearing Lucas moving around. Then a gentle touch between my thighs, a warm cloth gently cleaning me and soothing over-sensitive tissues.

My head is lolling back against Tate's shoulder, and I can feel how hard he is beneath my ass. His fingers idly caress my stomach, and there's something so good about just lying here and letting both of them take care of me.

It makes me feel wanted in a way I haven't felt for ten years. A way I haven't let myself feel since before I left Tate.

"Pretty little sub," Lucas murmurs, his deep voice warm. "You tasted delicious. You're such a good girl for me and Master Tate."

I shiver and glance at him from beneath my lashes. He's still kneeling between my thighs, amber gaze on mine. "Thank you, Daddy," I say, and for the first time, I actually mean it. The gold in his eyes flares, and I realize that I've pleased him, and more, I *like* that I've pleased him.

Lucas kneels upright, lifting his hand and cupping my cheek, his thumb brushing over my skin. Then he leans in and covers my mouth with his in a kiss that takes me by surprise. I go still as his hand slides from my cheek and into my hair, cupping the back of my head, his tongue pushing into my mouth. I shudder, tasting myself as Lucas deepens the kiss, turning it hot and slow and sweet.

Then I feel Tate's lips against my nape, the brush of his beard against my skin, the light touch of his fingers on my back, tracing lazy circles as he presses yet more kisses to my shoulders.

They're hard these men, and yet their touch is gentle, and I'm shivering with pleasure under the press of Lucas's mouth and Tate's caressing hands. But it's not desperate this time. It's slow and easy, and I feel as if I could sit here all day, being kissed by Lucas and touched by Tate.

But then Lucas pulls away, and he rises to his feet. "Kneel here," he says, pointing to a spot on the carpet. "Eyes on the floor, little one."

"Yes, Daddy," I reply obediently.

Tate lets me go, and I slide off his lap, moving on shaking legs to the spot Lucas indicated, then kneeling. I have no idea what's going to happen next, but anticipation is coiling in my gut, along with a healthy dose of trepidation.

Tate gets up from the armchair and goes to the drinks cabinet, getting out the bottle again, and pouring them both another measure of vodka. Then he murmurs something to Lucas that I can't quite hear.

My heart rate kicks up a notch, and I suck in a shuddering breath. I hear the rustle of clothes, and suddenly Tate is in front of me, going down on his knees. He's gotten rid of his shirt, and I can't help but gape at his bare chest and shoulders. Broader than he was ten years ago, and more muscular, crisp hair and velvety tanned skin. He's so beautiful, my heart aches.

His green eyes hold mine, fierce and intense. He reaches out and grabs me by the hips, urging me to kneel upright as he pulls me close against him. My bare breasts brush his chest, my nipples hardening at the heat of his skin. "Keep still," he says, his gaze searching mine. "Trust us."

My heart rate increases, thudding in my ears. "Yes, Sir," I whisper, and realize I do trust them. Whatever happens now, I trust them completely.

Then I feel the warmth of Lucas behind me, his hands on the inside of my thighs urging them apart. I tremble a little as I shift my position, and then I feel his hand at my ass, his fingers slipping between my cheeks, something cold and liquid on them. I gasp as his fingers push, finding the tight entrance and pushing against it. Tate's large, warm palms are on my hips, steadying me as Lucas works his finger in and out.

"You're going to take both of us," Tate says. "And it'll hurt at first, then it'll feel good. But again, sub. You can't come until we give you permission."

I tense as shock echoes through me. Both of them? At once? "S-sir," I stutter, breathing fast. "I've never done that before and I—"

"Ssh." Tate puts an uncharacteristically gentle hand against my cheek. "We have. We know what we're doing, okay? All you have to do is relax and let us do all the work."

Which is what he promised me at the beginning of all this. Submission is a gift, he said, a gift of trust, and I know that the trust I gave them both ten years ago hasn't gone anywhere. It's still there. I mean, it must be. I wouldn't have gone behind the curtain and into that hallway with Tate, otherwise.

No, it's not them I don't trust, it's myself. My feelings of shame around my sexuality have been ingrained for a long time, but I'm tired of them. There's nothing dirty or wrong about this, about being with them, and I know that, because they're not ashamed. And I do trust them. I do.

So, I relax against Lucas's gentle finger as he spreads the lube around, and then when he's done, I hear him roll on a condom. Then it's his hands on my hips, pulling me back against him, and I feel his bare skin on mine, as hot as Tate's. I'm shaking at the touch, feeling the oiled silk of his skin, and the length of his cock slipping between my ass cheeks. Tate watches me intently as I feel Lucas push against my ass and then in. He's so big and I've never had sex there before, and it's painful, making tears spring in my eyes.

"That's it," Tate murmurs, never taking his gaze from mine. "Take him, sub. Take all of him."

I pant as Lucas eases deeper, going slowly, carefully, and I want to take all of him. I want to. I want to take both of them, because I owe them. I know that now. I ran from them, ran from my hunger and my desire, and I was wrong not to explain. Not to give them even a hint of an explanation or a choice.

I groan as Lucas sinks into me, his groin right up against my ass, his breathing harsh in my ear. "Such a good girl," he says softly, brushing his mouth over my bare shoulder. "Tight and hot. Perfect for Daddy."

I let myself lean back against him, into his heat, shuddering with pleasure at the approval in his voice, and the gravel, too. I'm affecting him, making him want, and a strange feeling sweeps through me.

Both of these beautiful men want me. Not just anyone, *me*. And that gives me a power I hadn't realized I had before.

Tate moves closer, undoing his pants and rolling a condom down with easy, deliberate movements. Then he's right up against my front, my breasts pressed to his chest as he guides himself into me.

It's overwhelming at first, the two of them stretching me.

I feel there's no room for anything, no room for breath, no room for me, and I shudder, groaning as Tate pushes deeper. Then I'm sandwiched between the two of them. One wall of hard, hot muscle at my back, the other pressed up against my front.

"That's it," Tate says, his voice deeper, harsher. "Your pussy is perfect too." Then he bends his head and his mouth takes mine, a hungry kiss, ravaging me, conquering me. And they begin to move, both of them in sync, a slow back and forth, in and out, that makes me pant and gasp against Tate's lips.

It hurts at first, and it's as uncomfortable as Tate said it would be, but then the pressure turns into a steadily building pleasure, and I want to move. But Tate growls against my mouth, "Keep still, sub." His hands are on my hips, making sure I stay exactly where I am, while Lucas reaches around to cup one breast, his fingers pinching and rolling my nipple.

I pant as they stay slow, a pull and a push, an in and out, and I'm caught between them, held and contained by them in the most perfect way.

This is all for me, and it's too intense. I can't bear it, yet I want to be worthy of this. To be worthy of them and how they stayed true all these years, while I did not. So, I hold on to the orgasm, and I resist it, even as Tate keeps kissing me, keeps moving inside me, and Lucas squeezes my breasts gently.

The sensations are too much, the pleasure too intense, and again I feel that strange panic. I don't want to disappoint them. "Please," I whisper against Tate's mouth. "Please let me come. I don't want to disappoint you, not again."

"You'll never disappoint us, sweet girl," he murmurs.

"Never," Lucas whispers, nuzzling in my ear.

"Come for us," Tate says.

"Both of us," Lucas murmurs.

Then Tate reaches down, and his fingers stroke my clit at the same time as Lucas pushes deep, and the friction is too much. It's all too much. Pleasure explodes, and I put my head back, screaming at the ceiling as it moves relentlessly through me like a bomb blast.

I'm held there, barely conscious as I feel the pair of them move in sync, one in my pussy, one in my ass, harder, deeper, and then Tate growls, his teeth against my lip, and Lucas's teeth close on my shoulder as the pair of them follow me over the edge.

For long moments afterwards, I rest there, caught between the two of them, the most wonderful feeling washing through me. Of being held and cared for and cherished.

Eventually, the pair of them move, pulling out of me carefully. I slump back against Lucas, his warm chest a perfect place to rest. Tate says something, but I'm not paying attention, and it's clearly not for me anyway, since Lucas responds, his voice deep and caressing.

There's movement, and I'm in Lucas's arms as he carries me over to the armchair. He sits with me in his lap once more, and my legs are spread, and there is warmth between them, Tate cleaning me up with that warm cloth.

He and Lucas murmur things to each other, but I have my eyes closed and I don't want to pay any attention. I want to rest here and not think for a bit.

Then I hear the door open and close, and a silence falls.

"Katie," Lucas says. "Look at me."

Katie. I'm always Katie to him, never Katherine.

I don't want to look at him, self-conscious all of a

sudden. Without Tate here, it feels forbidden to be naked with him, to be sitting here in his arms.

His fingers are beneath my chin, gripping me gently. "Katie."

Finally, I open my eyes and look up at him. His gaze is hypnotic, amber and gold, and burning. "What?" I ask, and it comes out more defensive than I wanted it to.

"Tate left so we can talk," he says.

13

Lucas

She's lying in my lap, so perfectly, beautifully naked, her red hair spilling over my shoulder and the arm of the chair. Her eyes are the blue of a summer sky, but there's a guarded expression in them.

She has a right to be guarded. Things between us were

confusing when she left, and I didn't make the situation any easier with that fucking kiss.

I even thought she might say her safe word when I walked in, especially given the shock on her face, but she didn't say it. And when I ordered her to stand in front of me, she did.

Fuck, no scene was ever as hot as the one I just had with her. Finally getting to touch her, to stroke her, to have her writhe in my arms, and then when I finally pushed inside her, feeling her pussy pulse around my cock as she came...

Everything I ever wanted. Everything I've ever fantasized about.

Including the way she's lying against me now, all lax and warm, and sated.

I told Tate that I wanted to talk to her, and he didn't protest. He knows how things stand with me when it concerns her, but I'm surprised he didn't even make a comment. He just went out of the room, leaving me space to talk without him, and I'm not sure what that means, but I'll have to think about it later. Right now, she's here, and there are things we need to say to each other.

"Are you okay with this?" I ask, her soft skin warm beneath my fingertips. "With me, I mean."

"Well, if I weren't, I would have said my safe word," she replies.

It's not the answer I was hoping for, then again, I have only myself to blame for that. And that's the reason I wanted to talk to her, to fix things between us, and if not for her, then for Tate at the very least.

"I'd like to tell you that I'm sorry for that kiss," I tell her. "But I'm not. What I *am* sorry for is how it complicated things with you and Tate."

She stares at me for a second, then her lashes lower, veiling her gaze. Hiding from me, the way she hides from Tate. "That's okay," she says. "You didn't complicate it."

"Katie," I order softly. "Look at me."

She sighs. "Why?"

"Because you're hiding, and I think we're both done with that, aren't we?"

Her lashes quiver. "Are we?"

"I've tasted you," I say, patient. "I've been inside you. And now you're naked in my lap. Don't you think hiding now is a bit like shutting the barn door after the horse has bolted?"

She shifts in my lap, the tension in her body apparent. She might not have resisted my dominance, but she's resisting my attempt at an honest conversation, and I'm not sure why. No, fuck that. I *do* know why.

With gentle pressure, I force her chin up again, so she has to look at me, and I hold her gaze, looking deep into her blue, blue eyes. Then I bent my head and cover her mouth in a kiss like the one I gave her when she was in Tate's lap. Slow, hot, and sweet. He's too impatient with kissing, but I'm not. There's nothing like a slow, sensual kiss, taking my time to explore and to feel the sub relax under my mouth.

Katie remains tense, but only for a second. After a moment, her mouth opens beneath mine, welcoming me in. She tastes like summer, strawberries and cream, with a hint of something tart. Fucking perfect. I kiss her deeper, keeping things slow and easy, and all the tension leaves her body as she relaxes against me.

It's only then that I lift my mouth from hers, and this time when she looks up at me, her eyes are wide, the wariness gone. "You've been the most perfect little sub," I tell her. "And in return for the gift of your trust, I'll give you my honesty."

She doesn't speak, but a crease appears between her brows.

"I've wanted you from the moment I saw you," I continue. "The day that Tate brought you over to sit at our table in the high school cafeteria was the worst day of my life."

Her eyes widen in shock. "Why?"

"Because I couldn't have you. Tate saw you first." I let her see the truth in my gaze. "I wasn't going to poach on his territory, and he's my brother in every way but blood. And if I wanted to keep our relationship, I knew I was going to have to deal with my feelings for you myself. So, I did. But being your friend and nothing more was the hardest thing I've ever had to do in my life."

She blinks, her gaze roaming over my face as if I'm a stranger she's never seen before. "Seriously?" she asks, still sounding shocked.

"Come on, Katie," I say gently. "You must have known."

A blush stains her cheeks the prettiest pink. "I...suppose I had a feeling it might be like that."

I stroke her jaw with my thumb, unable to keep from touching her. "And I think you felt it too, didn't you?"

Her blush deepens, but this time she doesn't look away. "Yes," she says starkly. "I did. And I'm not sorry about that kiss either."

Something tight and hot gathers in my chest, a savage kind of satisfaction. "Did you leave because of that?" I ask, the question I've been wanting to ask for years. "Because of what happened between us?"

She hesitates a moment, then says, "Partly. You were a complication that I didn't see coming, and you...confused me. I didn't understand how I could want two men."

That makes sense. We were all so young back then, still

trying to work out who we were as adults, and then with the added complication of my and Tate's shitty childhoods. Having a woman we both wanted in the center of everything was...difficult.

"So, you left?"

"So, I left," she agrees.

"You should have talked to us," I say, because I've been wanting to tell her this for years, too. "You should at least have told us why you were leaving."

She pulls her chin from my grip all of a sudden, glancing away. "I know," her voice sounds husky. "I should have. But I didn't want to have that conversation. I didn't want to tell Tate that I had feelings for you, because I didn't want to come between you two. And I thought you both would come after me if I said anything, and I didn't want you to."

I let her have her privacy for a minute, because this is a difficult conversation to have, and while both Tate and I were furious when she left, time and maturity have dulled our anger, or certainly mine at least.

"I was a coward," she says at last.

"No," I say, gathering her close. "You weren't a coward. You were nineteen and very young, and fuck, that's not a conversation any nineteen-year-old wants to have."

She turns her head into my chest. I've got my shirt back on, but I didn't do up the buttons, so her cheek is warm against my bare skin, and the tight, hot thing in my chest gets tighter. "I know, but still, I should have. I should have been brave enough."

I let my fingers sift through her red curls, and they feel just as soft and silky as I thought they would. She feels just as soft and silky as I thought she would. Christ, having her naked and in my arms like this, admitting that she had feelings for me, feels so good, so right. I told Tate this might be a problem, and it is.

"Look, I'm not going to lie," I say. "Tate was furious and so was I, and yes, if you'd told us you were leaving, we would have done our damndest to stop you. But..." I pause. "That's done now. That's over. I'm not angry about it anymore, and Tate isn't either."

She lifts her head and looks up at me, her blue gaze open. "He sounded angry when he spanked me."

"He wasn't." I smile, because while she certainly threw herself into that scene, she's still very new. "That was all part of the scene."

"Oh." Her cheeks are pink. "Did he...ask you to join in?"

"Yes."

"And you said yes because...you wanted me?"

She asks the question hesitantly, as if she's not sure of the answer, which, after what we all did together, is a little ridiculous of her.

"Katie," I tell her. "I've never stopped wanting you."

"Why?" she asks. "Why me?"

An easy question to answer. "Because you're bright and intelligent, and funny and warm. You're beautiful and so fucking sexy, and you have the bravest heart."

She blinks, her eyes turning liquid. "I never knew."

"Now you do." I stroke her cheek lightly. "So, I've been honest about my feelings for you, now it's your turn to come clean."

She is silent for a moment, just staring up at me. Then at last, she says softly, "I've never stopped wanting you, either."

Satisfaction grips me, as well as a relief that really shouldn't be as intense as it is. "Is that why you didn't use your safe word?"

"Yes. Out in the hallway, when you were with the sub in that room, I came fantasizing about you fucking me."

"Tate told me that's what happened. That's partly why he asked me to join in."

She lifts a hand, and her fingertips brush my cheekbone, a light, almost hesitant touch as if she's not sure if she's allowed to. "What's the other part?"

"He didn't want to lose you," I say, and I'm sure Tate wouldn't mind me telling her this. It's not as if he's made any secret of it, after all. "And he didn't want to frighten you. He didn't want to push you too hard. We work well together as Doms since he's more of a hardass than I am, and he trusts me to tell him when he's going too far."

"Oh," she says, clearly thinking about this. "That makes sense." She frowns again. "Does he know....?"

"How I feel about you?" I finish. "Yes. He's always known."

More shock passes over her face, and with it, a clear expression of guilt. "I'm so sorry," she says. "I got between you two, and I hate—"

"No," I interrupt gently, but firmly. "You don't have to apologize. And you didn't get between us, not like that. He trusted me to deal with my feelings for you, to not let them get in the way of our friendship, and so that's what I did. I dealt with them." I don't add that a reckoning is going to come soon, and Tate and I both know it. "I've been dealing with them for years."

"That doesn't seem fair," she says, which makes my heart ache just a little bit.

"It is what it is. He's like a brother to me, and I couldn't let anything compromise that. I never had any siblings growing up in the foster system, or at least none that I stayed in touch with. Tate is the only real, lasting connection I have, and it's important to me."

Her fingertips graze the line of my jaw. "Will this change things?" she asks. "It will, won't it?"

Of course it will, and that's the problem.

It's going to change everything.

14

Tate

Lucas decided he wanted to talk to Katherine alone, and since I know it's the fair thing to do, I agreed. I've given them a good half an hour, and while I've been kicking my heels out in the bar, I've been thinking over things.

It was good with Katherine. Far, far too good. And it's only cemented my initial decision that she has to stay. And not only because of the pleasure I took in her submission and in the way she obeyed, but because I want *her*. I've missed her bright spirit in my life and the way she would never let me brood over things. She brought joy and laughter into my life, and it's darker without her. It's always darker without her.

She's so fucking brave, too, not batting an eye as Lucas and I took her both at the same time, and loving every second of it. But what sticks in my mind is her weeping, apologizing for leaving, and not telling us she was going.

I already know that there's more to this than she's letting on, and the time has come for some real answers. I don't want this — whatever it is—getting between us again. I need to know the answers and I need them now, because I have some decisions to make. Lucas made his position very clear when I asked him to join Katherine and me in a scene. Once he's had her, he's not going to let her go easily, and I know exactly where he's coming from.

Neither of us wants to give her up. But Lucas is my brother, the only one I ever had, and that connection is as important to me as it is to him. It's a pity we both prefer women, really, or that he isn't a sub, because that could work out well.

There's only one solution to the problem, though, and the more I think about it, the more attractive it becomes. A way I can keep them both. Of course, it'll be dependent on them, but I'm okay with it.

Strange, considering I'm possessive as fuck. Then again, watching Lucas with Katherine didn't make me jealous. No, it was the opposite, in fact. Hot as hell. He was good with her, gentle when she needed gentleness, and helped me when she needed a firm hand. The whole scene worked so perfectly, and having her with him at the end...

Perhaps that's what was missing all those years ago.

Katherine and I needed him to work, but back then, we didn't even know ourselves, let alone each other. Lucas and I both know who we are now and accept it, but Katherine doesn't. Or at least, not so far. She will with Lucas and my help, though, and I think she needs us. I think she needs *both* of us.

After the half hour has passed, I make my way back to my office, opening the door without announcing myself. They'll both know it's me, and if they're doing something they shouldn't, then all the better for me. I'd love to watch her go down on him, for example. A reversal of her sucking me while Lucas fucked her. This time she can suck him, while I sink into her perfect little pussy.

Sadly, they're not doing anything they shouldn't. Lucas is sitting in the armchair, and she's still in his lap. They look up as I come in, but don't say anything as I move over to the armchair opposite and sit down.

"You talked?" I ask into the heavy silence.

"Yes," Lucas says. "We cleared a few things up."

"Good," I say. "Come here, Katherine."

Lucas releases her, and slowly she slides off his lap, crossing the space between the armchairs to come and stand in front of mine. She looks as if she's standing in front of a firing squad, which does not amuse me.

"I'm not going to yell at you, sweet girl," I say mildly. "Don't look as if you're preparing to be shot."

A flush creeps through her cheeks. "I-I'm sorry, Tate."

I hold out my arms to her. "Come here."

She doesn't hesitate, coming close so I can pull her onto my lap. She's warm and soft, and achingly lovely.

"I missed you," I say, threading my fingers through her lovely red curls. "I've missed you for ten years."

She blinks up at me, her eyes filling with tears. "I was

just saying to Lucas that I shouldn't have left the way I did," she says thickly. "I should have been braver. I should have had the conversation with you both, but I didn't. I didn't know how to even say it."

"Say what?" I have an idea, but I'd like to hear it from her.

"What I felt for you." Her wide blue gaze meets mine. "I was the problem. I was the one who couldn't deal with wanting you and wanting Lucas, too. I was afraid of my own desires. I thought...it would be better for you if I just left. But it was never about you. It was about me."

I push a curl behind her ear. "Hate to break it to you, sweet girl, but it wasn't all you. I have to take the blame too, because you weren't the only one who couldn't deal with their desires. I thought I'd frightened you away."

"No," she says, then pulls a face. "I mean, yes, okay, you did frighten me. But not in the way you think." She swallows and looks away, and I allow her that because confessing can be hard when someone's watching, and we're not in a scene now. "You know, there's something else I haven't told you. Mom spent a lot of time drinking and picking up men. I'd wake up in the morning to find strange guys in the kitchen, which wasn't great." Her cheeks have gotten pinker and she's biting her lip. This is hard for her, I can see that.

Lucas pushes himself out of the armchair and goes to the drinks cabinet, calmly pouring out some drinks while Katherine talks.

"When I was sixteen," she goes on. "I came out of my bedroom one morning to find one of her hookups from the night before in the kitchen. He was younger than her usual, and hot, and he flirted with me a bit as I was getting my breakfast. I mean, at the time I thought he was just making conversation, but it was only later that I realized he was flirting. Anyway, I was getting some milk for my cereal, and when I turned around to put the bottle back in the fridge, he was right in front of me. He pinned me against the wall, took my chin in his hand, and kissed me. I was shocked at first, since I'd only kissed a couple of boys before then, and they didn't do it like that. But then...." She takes a breath. "I knew it was wrong, and I didn't want him to do any of that. But... there was a moment when it was...hot. I liked him holding me, and I liked him pressing me against the table and just... taking what he wanted. Something else might have happened, but Mom came in, and when she saw us, she was furious. He got kicked out, but she was so mad at me. She called me a dirty little slut and told me not to flaunt myself in front of men."

Anger coils like a snake in my gut, at the man who took what he shouldn't have from my Katherine, and at her mother for slut shaming a sixteen-year-old. Fuck, if that man were here, he wouldn't be safe from Lucas and me, and as for her mother... Well, a good job that hard-faced, bitter woman isn't here either. She blamed Katherine for something that wasn't her fault, and I won't fucking have it.

"She's wrong," I growl. "It had nothing to do with you and everything to do with her, and that fucking prick who assaulted you. Because it *was an* assault, you know that, don't you?"

"Yes." Katherine looks at me, clear-eyed. "Intellectually. Yeah, Mom blamed me, and she shouldn't have, but there's always been this doubt in me. That because I liked it, there was something...I don't know. Wrong with me."

"Fuck's sake," I say. "There's absolutely nothing wrong with you, sweet girl. Nothing at all."

"But I didn't know that at the time," Katherine says. "And because she made me feel so ashamed of my sexuality, I kind of hated being turned on. Especially when you were being bossy."

And now I'm furious with myself. For knowing something was wrong at the time, because I certainly fucking knew, yet not being patient enough with her to get an answer. To give her space and time to tell me.

"Katherine," I say roughly. "I'm the one who owes you an apology. I should have been more careful. I should have—"

She reaches up and lays a finger across my lips, and I'm so surprised I actually shut up. "You didn't know, so how could you have been careful? I didn't tell you."

Lucas comes over with a tumbler of vodka for me and puts it on the side table next to the armchair. Then he strokes his fingers through Katherine's hair. "Oh, Katie," he says. "I'm so sorry that happened to you." His voice is gentle, but I see the fury flickering in his eyes.

Katherine takes her finger from my mouth and leans into Lucas's stroking hand. "I am, too. I thought it had warped my sexuality forever. And when I started having feelings for Luc, I thought I must be the slut my mother called me."

This time, I take her chin in my hand and tilt her head back, so her blue gaze is on mine. "Firstly, I don't care if you're a slut or not," I say flatly and emphatically. "Secondly, your mother was a bitch to say what she did, and she's wrong. There's nothing wrong with your sexuality, and there is nothing wrong with you."

She looks fiercely up at me. "You really think so?"

"I wouldn't lie to you, Katherine. I'm kinky as fuck and many people would call that wrong, but I don't give a shit. We are what we are, and what you are is brave and strong as hell. Submission is a strength because you hold all the cards. You're the one who can make us or break us, and my sweet Katherine, you made Lucas and me feel like gods tonight."

"It's true." Luc crouches down beside the armchair. "You're something special, Katie. And you should know that."

She glances at him, then up at me, and she smiles. "I mean, I do feel special when I'm with you two. I don't think I ever have before."

I know what she needs now, and when I give Lucas a quick look, I see agreement in his eyes. If no one has ever made her feel special before, then it's up to us to make her feel as if she's the most precious thing in the entire universe.

He lifts his glass and takes a sip. Then he leans forward and takes Katherine's mouth in another of his long, slow kisses. He really loves a kiss, and this one is extra special, because it's got alcohol in it.

Katherine gives a little gasp, then a moan as she drinks from Lucas's mouth. And when he lifts his head, her cheeks are pink, and her eyes are glittering like stars.

Pretty, pretty little sub.

"Go and lie on the floor, sub," I say softly, pointing to the soft rug between the armchairs.

She moves quickly, sliding out of my lap and going over to the spot I indicated, lying down on her back. Then Lucas and I move over there, too. He kneels above her head, taking it between his hands and tilting it up and back. Then he covers her mouth again in another kiss, while I start at the other end, spreading her thighs so I can kneel between them. I slide my hands beneath her ass and lift her, so her pussy is right there, glistening and soft and luscious, and I lick straight up the middle of her. She jerks, gasping into Lucas's mouth, giving me the sweetest reaction. So, then I settle in. Because I've been waiting ten years for a taste of this pussy, and I'm going to take my time.

She's delicious, all sweet and salty, and she gasps and jerks beneath my tongue as I slide it all the way into her wet heat.

Lucas lifts his mouth from hers and then kneels behind her, lifting her head and shoulders in his lap. "Look," he murmurs, cupping the back of her head in his palms and raising it so she can see me between her thighs. "He loves the way you taste."

Her cheeks are flushed red, and her eyes are dark with pleasure as they meet mine. I hold her gaze as I continue to lick her fucking delicious little cunt, letting her know exactly how much I'm loving eating her.

She groans, lifting her hips to my mouth and shifting around, her whole body trembling as I push her higher and higher.

"This is for you, Katie," Lucas says softly. "Come when you want."

Of course, she can, but I draw it out as much as I'm able, because I want to give her the maximum amount of pleasure I can, show her exactly what she is worth, which is everything. So, I edge her and edge her and edge her until she's arching against the carpet, moaning as loud as she can, and I love that too.

Then I give her one last flick of my tongue, and she screams as she comes, her orgasm tasting sweet on my tongue.

15

Katherine

I'm lying on my back, every part of me still shaking with the aftershocks. Tate nuzzles against my inner thigh, the prickle of his beard on my sensitive skin making me shiver. Lucas is looking down at me, his amber gaze full of heat, and I can't look away.

I can't stop thinking about that conversation we had before Tate walked in, either. About how he wanted me from the moment he first saw me, and my poor heart can't deal with how good that makes me feel. Even if there's a sharp ache there too, because feeling the same way about him is wrong. I love Tate, I always have, but loving Lucas, too, is out of the question. You can want two men, but loving two men? It just doesn't work, no matter how accepting either of them are of my sexuality. I can have tonight at least, that's allowed, and so I'll take advantage of it to the fullest.

I lift my hands to Lucas's face, taking it between my palms. "Let me do something for you," I murmur, because I want to. I know he feels guilty about how things were between us years ago, but I want him to know that he doesn't need to. "Let me make you feel good."

"You already have, sweetheart," he says.

The endearment makes my heart feel too full. "No," I say. "I want to do something especially for you."

"This isn't about me, though. It's about you."

"Let her," Tate says roughly. "If this is about her, then we have to accept her wishes."

"See?" I stroke the side of his face with my thumbs. "You have to now."

His golden eyes flare, the lines of his face hard and set. He wants this, I can see it, but he also doesn't want me to know how badly. Or maybe he doesn't want Tate to know. Then again, Tate knows already, doesn't he? And he's fine with it otherwise he wouldn't have told him to let me.

So, I turn over and kneel before him, reaching for the button of his pants to undo it, then slowly easing his zipper down. He's hard and ready for me, so I take him out. His long, thick cock feels like steel and velvet in my hands, and when I stroke him, the breath hisses between his teeth.

I bend and take him in my mouth, licking the head of his dick, loving the hitch in his breathing as I do. Then I close my lips around him, swallowing him as deeply as I can, gripping him hard.

"Fuck, yes," he breaths, his fingers sliding into my hair. But not to guide me. He's letting me be in charge of this, so I play. Licking and nipping, then working him in my mouth, letting him know that I think he's beautiful.

His fingers tighten as I swallow him even deeper, so he's pushing against the back of my throat, but I don't stop. And then I feel Tate behind me, his hands on my hips, tipping me forward a bit. He strokes the curves of my ass then eases his fingers between my thighs, where I'm still slick from his tongue. A moan escapes me, the vibration of it, making Lucas's jaw go tight.

"Look at him," Tate orders. "Look at him while you're sucking him."

So, I do, meeting Lucas's amber gaze, full of fire and heat, gasping as I feel Tate push into me from behind. Tate goes slow, but I'm still shaking from the previous orgasm. Yet it's not too much. It's not too much at all as I gaze up at Lucas, and I can see how much this is turning him on, how much he actually wants me, and with him in my mouth and Tate behind me, inside me, I feel a connection to both of them, and it's not just physical, it's deeper than that.

There's an emotional connection between us — between all of us. Me for Lucas and Tate. Tate for Lucas and me. Lucas for me and Tate. It's real and it's intense, and maybe it's always been there, and we were just too young to handle it.

Whatever our connection is, though, this is only for a night, and I have to remember that, even as the taste of Lucas sits on my tongue, and the feel of Tate behind me drives my pleasure into the stratosphere. Lucas thrusts harder into my mouth, and I can see by the intense glow of his eyes that he's nearly there, his jaw tightening. He looks beautiful like this, and I'm desperate to see what he looks like when he comes, because he's been behind me before. Tate's fingers grip my hips firmly, his thrusts getting harder, faster. "Come with him," he growls and I'm pretty much on the verge of doing so already.

So, I suck harder, my gaze held captive by Lucas's, and I feel Tate's hand reach around and his fingers slide between my thighs, finding my clit and stroking in time with his thrusts. And as the orgasm begins to explode through me, I see Lucas's eyes glitter bright gold. "Fuck, Katie," he murmurs, and then he's coming at the same time, with me groaning around his cock as he empties himself down my throat. And I'm still in the throes of it when Tate pulls me back against him, so I'm upright on my knees with him behind me, still thrusting into me. His arms are iron bands around me, holding me tight as he drives himself inside me, and when I feel his body tense, he takes my jaw in his hand and turns my head to my shoulder, twisting me so he can kiss me, and he does, thrusting deep into my pussy even as his tongue is in my mouth, making me take his growl of release as he comes too.

He shudders against me, his kiss raw and savage, and then he keeps a tight hold on me as he takes his mouth away, pressing his face against my hair. I feel his warm breath against the back of my neck, and my heart aches.

I have missed him. I've missed the feel of his arms around me. No other man has ever made me feel the way I feel right now, powerful, strong, and special. So very special. Well, no other man except Lucas.

After a moment, Tate pulls out of me, going down on his knees and taking me with him so I'm sitting on his powerful thighs. He's big and hot and hard behind me, yet this time his hands are gentle on my hips, stroking me as his breathing calms.

Lucas does his pants up and then comes over to where Tate and I are, crouching down in front of me. His amber gaze is direct. "Thank you, sweetheart," he says. "Thank you for tonight. You were a gift."

My chest goes tight. "It's okay," I say thickly. "So were you."

He smiles, and that makes my chest feel even tighter, because his smiles make him even more beautiful. "I'm going to order us some food, because all this exercise is making me hungry." He flicks a glance behind me. "You hungry, Tate?"

"Yeah, good plan," Tate says.

After Lucas leaves the room, Tate shifts me, and I sit on the floor as he deals with the condom and does his pants up. Then he comes back to where I'm sitting and picks me up in his arms, carrying me back to the armchair again.

"You okay?" he asks, looking down into my eyes with a concerned expression.

"Oh yes," I say. "I'm more than okay, actually."

His expression relaxes and his mouth curves in a smile. He's beautiful when he smiles, too. "You talked with Luc?"

"I did."

"All good?"

"Yes. We sorted some things out." I shiver slightly, and he leans down to pick up the woolen throw that's folded up neatly on the floor, and wraps me up in it.

"Just as well," he says, his arms tightening around me. "Because I'm not letting you go, okay? Not now."

I go still, staring up at him. "What? What do you mean?"

"You came here." His green eyes glitter. "You came back to me, and I don't intend to let you go again."

Something cold winds through me, despite the heat of his body and the throw wrapped around me. "Tate," I say, a slight husk in my voice. "One night doesn't mean forever. I never intended to—"

"I know you didn't," he interrupts. "But I always meant to find you, Katherine. It's been ten years, and now it's time to come home."

He's so peremptory, so sure of himself, and I can see the intent blazing in his eyes. He means this. But it didn't work the last time, and there's no reason it'll work this time either, even now my secret's out.

"I said a night, Tate," I say flatly. "That's all."

"A night is not enough," he says, his tone flat as mine. "I want more. And I think you want more, too."

I push myself abruptly out of his arms, wrapping the throw around me and going over to the armchair opposite. Then I sit down on it, needing some distance. He doesn't make any attempt to stop me, but he's staring at me now, his rough, handsome features set in hard lines. He's even more uncompromising than he used to be, and just as difficult to say no to.

"What is it about being with me that scares you?' he asks into the silence."

I have to be honest with him. I can't lie, not anymore. "It didn't work before," I tell him. "You and me. What's to say that'll work now?"

"It's been ten years, Katherine," Tate says, impatient. "I've changed, and so have you. But you have to know, I loved you then and I love you still, and I want us to try again."

A little shock goes through me. He loves me. Still? After all these years?

And you still love him. You always have.

I look away, unable to bear his gaze, my heart aching. I could go back to him, it's true. But... what if I'm not enough for him now? I was back then, but if he's changed, so have I, and what he wants...I'm not sure I can give it to him. And then there's Lucas...

"Tate, I—"

At that moment, Lucas comes back in, his sharp amber gaze taking in the distance between Tate and me. "Food will be coming," he says. "What's going on?"

"I've told Katherine that I don't want to let her go again," Tate says baldly.

I don't look at either of them, my gaze instead on the throw. It has a fringe and I'm toying with it. I don't want to have this conversation in front of Lucas. It feels unfair. "We should have this conversation at another time," I say. "Don't spoil tonight."

"No," Tate says. "We'll have this conversation here, right now."

Lucas is silent for a moment. Then he says, "You and I need to talk, Tate." His tone is hard and just as uncompromising as Tate's. "Katie doesn't need to be here to listen."

My heart becomes even more painful. I don't want to be the reason for these two to argue. I can't bear the thought of all this complication yet again.

But then Tate says, "We don't have to make this hard. We can make this easy."

"What's easy?" Lucas asks sharply.

Tate stares at him. "You. Me. And her. All of us. Together. We're family. That's what we are, what we've always been."

Shock ripples through me, and I can't help staring open-mouthed at Tate. "What do you mean together?" I demand.

His sharp green gaze comes to mine. "You're ours,

Katherine. And I think tonight has shown us that we can make it work. It's good, all of us together. It's really good."

Lucas is staring at him, too. "What the fuck are you talking about?"

He pushes himself out of his chair and stands, facing Lucas, meeting his gaze head-on. "You love her, Luc. You've always loved her, and so do I. But I'm not going to make her choose."

"What if I don't want either of you?" I can't help saying, a weird thing happening in my gut. "What if all I wanted was a night? Did you even think to ask me?"

A muscle jumps in the side of his strong jaw, because, of course, he didn't think to ask me. He's a man used to getting what he wants, and that includes me. The thought that I might not choose him or want what he's offering has clearly never occurred to him.

Lucas is staring at Tate, too, his expression unreadable. Neither of them has heard what I said. Angry now, I get up from my armchair, letting the throw fall to the ground. Then I go over to the table where my clothes are still neatly stacked, and I start getting dressed.

"What are you doing?" Lucas asks, finally noticing me.

"I'm getting dressed. What does it look like?" I pull up my skirt, then put my shirt on, fastening the buttons. "Then I'm going to go home."

But then Lucas moves over to where I'm standing and puts one hand very deliberately on the door. "No, you're not."

Then, as if he's reading Lucas's mind, Tate comes to stand behind me, the pair of them making sure I can't go forward or back.

I look up at Lucas, my throat tightening. "Let me go."

"No," he says. "Tate's right, we decide right now, right here. All of us together."

I let out a breath, then glance behind me, up at Tate. He's staring down at me, and behind the insistence and demand in his eyes, I can see the edges of desperation. "I can't lose you again, Katherine," he says quietly, as vulnerable and as open as he's ever going to be. "Please don't walk away."

"What about this that bothers you, Katie?" Lucas asks, his voice warm and soft.

I turn back to him, and I swallow. They have been honest with me this whole time, and they deserve the same from me.

Lucas is looking down at me, and I can feel Tate's gaze too, and it's like standing between two giant redwoods, yet not in a bad way. It feels protective, as if I'm being held safe and cared for.

"It didn't work out last time," I say, my voice hoarse. "And that was because of me. And you're both...so incredible, and I just..." I swallow. "What if I'm not enough?"

Lucas frowns. "I think tonight should have told you that you're more than enough for both of us."

"Yes," Tate says. "Don't ever think you're not."

I know they mean it. I can hear it in their voices. Having both of them, and this time without all the fear and the toxicity. All knowing how each other feels and knowing that it's okay.

Tate's hands gently come to rest on my shoulders, near the base of my neck, and the pressure feels good. It feels like ownership, and that's something I never thought I'd want, but I like it.

Lucas glances at Tate over my shoulder, and something wordless passes between them. Then he puts his hands over

Tate's so I'm wearing a necklace of warm skin and warm fingers, a collar that makes me feel claimed.

"I don't want you to be jealous," I say thickly. "I don't want either of—"

"We're possessive motherfuckers, it's true," Tate interrupts. "But I don't want to lose you, and I don't want to lose him."

Lucas nods, looking down at me. "This is what we both want, Katie." Then he looks at Tate, and as one, they lift their hands from me. "But only if you want it too."

I don't like the way I feel suddenly cold at the loss of their touch. And I don't like the way my heart is aching and aching.

I could have both of them. I don't have to choose. And it's not wrong. *I'm* not wrong. So why not try again? If we start with honesty and build from there, where's the harm?

And we could build something truly beautiful together, I know we could.

So, I go up on tiptoes and press my mouth to Lucas's, then I turn and kiss Tate. And I reach for each of their hands, and I thread my fingers through theirs, holding on, the three of us creating a current that I don't think will ever fade.

"I want it," I say simply. "I want to try. Together, we're family."

"We are," Lucas agrees.

"Well." Tate lets out a breath. "Looks like I'm going to need a bigger bed."

EPILOGUE

Katherine

It's newbie night at The Club Manhattan, and Tate is going to give a demonstration, since I'm his sub, that includes me. I'm kneeling on the stage, waiting for him, with my wrists cuffed behind my back. I'm also naked.

I also don't care that I'm naked.

It's been a year since Tate, Lucas, and I created a little family together, and I can't remember when I've ever been happier. There were a few disagreements about our living situation, but eventually Tate and Lucas decided it would be easier if we all lived together, so that's what we did. We have a fabulous penthouse apartment in Downtown, with enough space for all of us to be private if we want to, and with big enough beds if we don't.

Despite my fears, it's working, it's really working. We're all honest with each other and we talk through stuff, and while there are arguments and issues – there always will be with two dominant men –- we always find a solution. We don't let things fester or become toxic.

Having them slowly introduce me to the BDSM scene was a little challenging initially, not to mention confronting, but I surprised myself. My boundaries aren't as fixed as I thought they'd be. I'm Lucas and Tate's sub, and we do scenes together at the club, and sometimes they include someone else. But the only men I want to fuck are them. There was some jealousy at first, mostly from me, because while Lucas only wants to fuck me, Tate doesn't. But I soon got over it. I know Tate's heart is mine, and so is Lucas's, and that's all I want.

The crowd in front of the stage is quiet as Tate approaches, all eyes glued to him, his dominance moving with him like a wave. I shiver in anticipation.

Tate loves an audience, and as it turns out, so do I, and this isn't the first time we've done a scene together in front of a crowd.

Right behind Tate comes Lucas, the quiet strength of his authority quietening the remaining whispers. Both of them get onto the stage and move over to where I'm kneeling, and I quickly lower my gaze to the floor in front of me.

Lucas touches my hair gently while Tate tests my cuffs.

"Ready, sweet girl?" Tate murmurs.

"Yes, Sir," I say.

Lucas's hand moves, and he grips the nape of my neck in a possessive hold. "Then let's begin," he says.

Enjoy this?
Try the other books in the Lessons in Dominance Series!

Hard Discipline by Jackie Ashenden
After Hours by Caitlin Crews
After Dark by Caitlin Crews
Bad Girl Dilemma by Zara Cox
Bound and Branded by Maisey Yates

Also in Kindle Unlimited by Jackie Ashenden:

Knight Takes Queen: A spicy chess romance

EXCERPT FROM HARD DISCIPLINE

Odette

The Uber drops me off right in front of the huge glass edifice that is The Clouds, Manhattan's newest and most exclusive hotel, and I hate it on sight. It's a monument to rich men and greed, and also it's kind of phallic. I'm sure a man designed it.

I struggle to pull down the hem of my too-short black dress as I get out of the car at the same time as I'm trying to balance on the cheap black patent heels I bought online a couple of years ago and never wear. I'm also second-guessing myself as to why I'm here, but hey, at least I *am* here. I've been working on my follow-through, which, and I'll be the first to admit, I'm not great at. But still, I'm out of my apartment so that's something.

My mom named me Odette after the princess in Swan Lake, which I do not love. It doesn't help that I have long pale hair and am built on the small side, so people think I'm either a victim or a princess—AKA too helpless to look after myself. Which isn't true. To be honest, I wish I was built taller, stronger, and more muscular than I am, but I'm a woman and we're never happy with the body we're born with. I could have gone to the gym, I guess, but that would involve being around strangers and I'm not good with strangers—so weak, with noodle arms, it is.

On the sidewalk outside the hotel, the doormen nod as I approach, and one holds the door open for me. I wonder who they think I am in my obviously cheap clothing. A sex worker, probably, though I'm not as well dressed as, say, a high-class escort would be. Still, I was told I'd be expected so at least I don't have to plead with them to let me in.

Inside, everything is black marble and gold, the reception desk a huge slab of the same black marble as the floor. A man sits behind it, wearing black, and as I open my mouth to say I'm an expected guest, he points me towards one of the elevators.

Okay then. I close my mouth and walk over to it, nervously clutching my glittery silver evening purse, which now feels like the wrong choice.

My God, I hate places like this, which is a little rich coming from someone currently dating the son of a billionaire, I know, but still. This is not my natural habitat and it shows. It makes me feel conspicuous, and if there's one thing I hate, it's feeling conspicuous.

The elevator doors open and I search the for button I need. The instructions said that I was to meet him in the Pinnacle Suite and sure enough, there's a button just for that suite. So I press it. The elevator doors close and we're moving.

So, okay, the reason I'm here is not for sex work (which is fine, I'm not judging), but sex. Just sex. I signed up to this app called The Club, which is kind of like a dating service for people into BDSM, and I've been matched with some guy called Master Six. This is what they term a "playdate" but obviously this kind of playdate isn't for kids.

I did a lot of research before deciding The Club was the way to go, so it wasn't like a spur of the moment thing. Sure, I don't know this guy from Adam — his bio was only a list of things he's into and there was no picture — which is usually a giant no from me, but The Club members are vetted and clinic visits are mandatory, so he's probably not a psycho. I kind of lied on my own bio, though. I said I was an experienced submissive, but I'm not. I've actually never done any BDSM before, so what I'm doing tonight is probably going to end up being a giant mistake, but oh well. *C'est la vie*. I'm not backing out, not now.

I was assaulted last year while I was in college (Yale if you must know). I was out with some girlfriends and I left the bar early because I needed to study, and I didn't notice the guy following me. He shoved me up against a wall and punched me in the face and then...yeah, it's all still a blur. Anyway, I've always been anxious, but the assault pushed my anxiety into a full blown panic disorder, and eventually I ended up dropping out of college. I was there on a scholarship, so that was a bummer, but even more so was the six months I spent in my apartment, not wanting to leave it. I'm much better now — I got some therapy and the panic attacks are under control — but I'm not where I want to be.

My relationship with my boyfriend, Lucas, isn't going well. He's a nice guy, but he didn't sign up to babysit a poor, frightened mouse, and I'm really conscious of that. He's never said anything, but ever since the assault he treats me as if I'm made of glass, and even though I told him he didn't need to, he still does. Especially in bed, which is where the main issue is. He touches me as if I might break, constantly asking me if I'm okay, which makes me *more* anxious not less. I feel as if he's the one who's not okay and I'm the one having to give him reassurance, which isn't fair, because he's trying. But still, it's not sexy for me and it makes it difficult to get lost in the moment.

Anyway, I wouldn't have done anything about it if it wasn't for Gideon Fairfax.

He's Lucas's dad and I met him for the first time last summer at the Fairfax Estate in the Hamptons. He's some kind of property billionaire, and Lucas has a problematic relationship with him, because after Lucas's mother died, his father basically pulled away and buried himself in work.

So far, so terrible, billionaire dad.

But that's not the worst part. The worst part, the really, *really*, like, terrible part, is that Lucas's dad is the hottest fucking man I've ever laid eyes on. I should also say *not including Lucas* but I can't say that because he's hotter than his son. He's got that older man vibe, where men kind of settle into their looks and what was once pretty, becomes harder, stronger, edgier. Also, he's just got this...aura about him. It's the confidence of a man at the top of his game, a man with money and power, a leader through and through. He has a presence, a charisma, a magnetism, a....

I don't know... Something that you can't put into words, that you can only feel.

Anyway, the day Lucas introduced me to him, Mr. Fairfax's startling blue eyes met mine and I forgot what I was going to say. I just stood there gawping at him like a fish trying to breathe air. He shook my hand, said something about being pleased to meet me, then asked me where I was from. I couldn't remember how to speak so he had to ask me twice. So fucking embarrassing. But I could have gotten used to him and his effect on me, if it hadn't been for the incident with the horse. Some girl was riding on the beach below the Fairfax estate and a dog startled her horse. Lucas and I had been sunbathing, and I'd looked up at the barking dog just as Mr. Fairfax was coming out of the water. So I had a front row seat to him taking control of the horse situation. He grabbed the reins and ran one large hand down its neck and flanks, his deep voice issuing firm orders. He was only in swimming trunks, but he may as well have been wearing a crown for all that impaired his air of command.

Meanwhile, I sat there, my mouth open, staring at the expanse of smooth, olive skin wet from the sea, the sunlight shining on the water sheening every perfect muscle of his body. And my God....what a body it was. I never knew anyone's dad could look like that, but Lucas's dad did.

That night, in bed with Lucas, I tried to get him to be a little firmer with me, tell me what he wanted me to do, that kind of thing, but he didn't understand. So I had to get myself off after he'd fallen asleep, guiltily imagining I was the skittish horse, with Mr. Fairfax's strong hands on me, his voice telling me what to do...

Anyway, months of fantasies and continually disappointing sex with Lucas later, things between us are going downhill fast, and I need to do something to fix it. I mean, the problem is me, and I can't tell Lucas what I want, because I don't really know.

Hence me signing up to The Club. I get off on dominating fantasies featuring Mr. Fairfax, so what I want by signing up is to find out if I'm actually submissive. And if I am, that means that I can tell Lucas what I need, instead of him trying to guess. But obviously I need someone experienced, someone I can trust, and that's why I got The Club app.

The elevator stops and the doors slide open, revealing a silent, peaceful looking sitting area with a low couch and a table with a single orchid artistically arranged in a glass vase. To the right as I step from the elevator car, is a door. A gold plaque on the wall beside it tells me that this is indeed the Pinnacle Suite and a book has been put between the door and the frame to stop it from closing.

He said the door would be open and I should just walk in.

I swallow, my anxiety getting worse as I stare at the door standing ajar.

I shouldn't have lied on my application form when I joined The Club. You're supposed to put in your bio if you're new to the scene, or only interested in exploring, but I didn't. Because the other reason I'm here is that I didn't want anyone to treat me like I'm made of glass or go easy on me. I want to feel strong, have someone silence the constant hum of anxiety in my brain, and maybe Master Six will do that for me. I fucking hope so, because if this doesn't work, I don't know what I'll do.

I keep staring at the door, not moving. Turns out that thinking a thing is fine, but when it comes time to doing it, then it's a whole different story. Still, I've managed to get myself this far, so falling at the first hurdle would be dumb.

I take a steadying breath and make myself walk through the front door of the suite, letting it close behind me.

It's deathly quiet inside. In front of me is a very short hallway, so I walk down it, my heart thumping, the heels of my pumps sinking into the thick, cream carpet. The whole place reeks of luxury on a level I can't even begin to imagine; clearly Master Six isn't short of cash.

I step out of the hallway and into a huge living area dominated by big plate glass windows. They're massive and since the curtains aren't drawn, all of Central Park rolls out before us like a thick dark carpet dotted with lights. The room itself has a chandelier hanging from the ceiling, the same thick cream carpet as the hall and a huge modular couch in pale velvet facing the windows. A gigantic TV hangs on one wall, with yet more seating in front of it, and on the opposite side of the room is a long sideboard with lots of shelves and drawers.

A man is standing in front of it with his back to me. He's pouring drinks. He's very tall and from the way the plain black cotton of his business shirt stretches across wide, muscular shoulders, he's clearly built. He's wearing black pants and I can't help but notice that his waist is narrow and his thighs powerful. His hair is short and black, and as he deals with the drinks, his movements are unhurried.

Interest flickers inside me. I didn't give much thought to what kind of guy Master Six would be, or whether he'd be hot. I was too busy overthinking my impulsive agreement to meet him. But now I'm here and so is he, and he looks like he should be in a boxing ring or maybe charging across a battlefield with an axe, and hell, I'm only human. I only hope he's as hot from the front as he is from the back.

He doesn't turn and he doesn't speak, though he must know I'm here, and my anxiety intensifies. I should announce myself, but I'm sure my voice will shake and that's not a great first impression. Besides, there's a strange familiarity to him that's tugging at me and I don't know why.

I frown, studying his powerful figure as he calmly drops ice cubes into one of the tumblers. No, I'm not sure what about him is familiar, and that's a good thing since no one knows what I'm doing right now and I don't want anyone to know, either. Especially not Lucas, because obviously this is cheating. Even though I'm doing it *for* him. For us, really. After all, it's not like I'm going to do this again. This is very definitely a one-time thing.

I finally muster up the courage to announce myself, since it seems this guy isn't going to say anything anytime soon, but as soon as I open my mouth, he says, "You're late." He drops more ice cubes into the second glass. They make a metallic clinking sound. "Take your clothes off then go and kneel by the windows."

His voice is deep, dark as night, with a roughness to it that strokes over my skin like a cat's tongue. It's familiar, so, *so* familiar, and the coldest of shocks go through me as I realize why.

It's Gideon Fairfax's voice. Which must mean that this man is Gideon Fairfax.

Lucas's dad.

Fuck.

I freeze. I'm dead. Deceased. Just completely inanimate. A husk. My brain is screaming, *It's fucking Lucas's fucking dad!* over and over.

It can't be him, it can't be. But what if it is? What do I do? Stay here? Run from the room screaming from the room like a fucking lunatic? A little of both?

I need to get out, move, disappear before he turns around, but he's turning and I know already that it's too late. My body tenses, ready to go, but it's as if everything has dropped into slo-mo as Gideon Fairfax finishes his turn, and yes, it's him.

And yes, I'm fucked.

Totally fucked.

ABOUT JACKIE

Jackie writes dark, emotional stories with alpha heroes who've just got the world to their liking only to have it blown wide apart by their kick-ass heroines.

She lives in Auckland, New Zealand. When she's not torturing alpha males and their gutsy heroines, she can be found drinking vodka martinis, reading anything she can lay her hands on, wasting time on social media, or knitting yet more sweaters she doesn't need.

www.jackieashenden.com

ALSO BY JACKIE ASHENDEN

You Are Mine

Kidnapped By The Billionaire

In Bed With The Billionaire

Motor City Royals

Dirty For Me

Wrong For Me

Sin For Me

Bad Boy Sheikhs (Ebook only)

Never Seduce A Sheikh

Never Refuse A Sheikh

Never Resist A Sheikh

Texas Bounty

Cold Hearted Sniper (formerly Take Me Deeper)

Make It Hurt (ebook only)

Take Me Harder (ebook only)

The Hitman Next Door

Big Bad Marine

Black Sheep Bounty Hunter

Tate Brothers (Billionaire Navy SEALS)

The Dangerous Billionaire

The Wicked Billionaire

The Undercover Billionaire

11th Hour (Romantic Suspense)

Raw Power

Total Control

Hard Night

Alaska Homecoming (sexy small town)

Come Home to Deep River

Deep River Promise

That Deep River Feeling

Small Town Dreams (NZ set small town)

Find Your Way Home

All Roads Lead To You

Right Where We Belong

Arcadia Series (erotic age-gap billionaire romance)

Tamed

Bought

Owned

Harlequin Dare (erotic romance)

Ruined

Destroyed

King's Price

King's Rule

King's Ransom

The Debt

Dirty Devil

Sexy Beast

Bad Boss

In the Dark

With The Lights On

Harlequin Presents

Demanding His Hidden Heir

Claiming His One Night Child

Crowned At the Desert King's Command

The Spaniard's Wedding Revenge

Promoted to His Princess

The Most Powerful of Kings

The Italian's Final Redemption

The World's Most Notorious Greek

The Innocent Carrying His Legacy

The Wedding Night They Never Had

Pregnant by the Wrong Prince

The Innocent's One Night Proposal

A Diamond for My Forbidden Bride

Stolen for My Spanish Scandal

The Maid The Greek Married

Wed For Their Royal Heir

Her Vow To Be His Desert Queen

Novellas

Series

Billionaire's Club NYC (Ebook only)

The Billion Dollar Bachelor

The Billion Dollar Bad Boy

The Billionaire Biker

Boxed set of above: 100 Shades Hotter edition

Billionaire Fairy Tales (Ebook only)

The Billionaire's Virgin

The Billionaire Beast

The Billionaire's Intern

The Big Bad Billionaire

Multi-author series

Hollywood Blackmail (Seacliff Medical series)

Hold Me Down (Deacons of Bourbon Street biker series)

Frankie (Secret Confessions: Down and Dusty)

A Cowboy For All Seasons

A Good Old Fashioned Cowboy

Sweet Home Cowboy

The Comeback Cowboy

Lessons in Dominance

Hard Ride

Hard Discipline

The Bad Girl Dilemma (Zara Cox)

After Hours (Caitlin Crews)

After Dark (Caitlin Crews)

Bound and Branded (Maisey Yates)

Printed in Dunstable, United Kingdom